William Tell

Also by Travis Myers

&

Natasha Myers Marsiguerra

Sister Margaret

Hayden Jon Marshall

Jenny Black

Li Jun

Sol Abramowitz

William Tell

A Tommy Keane Novel

Travis Myers &
Natasha Myers Marsiguerra

Published in the United States by Bully Press Corp.
Bully Press Corp
P. O. Box 404
Wingdale, NY 12594 United States
 www.bullypress.net
Cover design by: Phred Rawles

ISBN-13: 978-1-7343370-3-7

For our dear mother and biggest fan, you will be missed.

***

Dedicated to every Cop and Detective, in every city, in every country on the planet. Thank you for standing on the side of right, and for fighting the good and never-ending fight against those who would destroy all we hold dear.

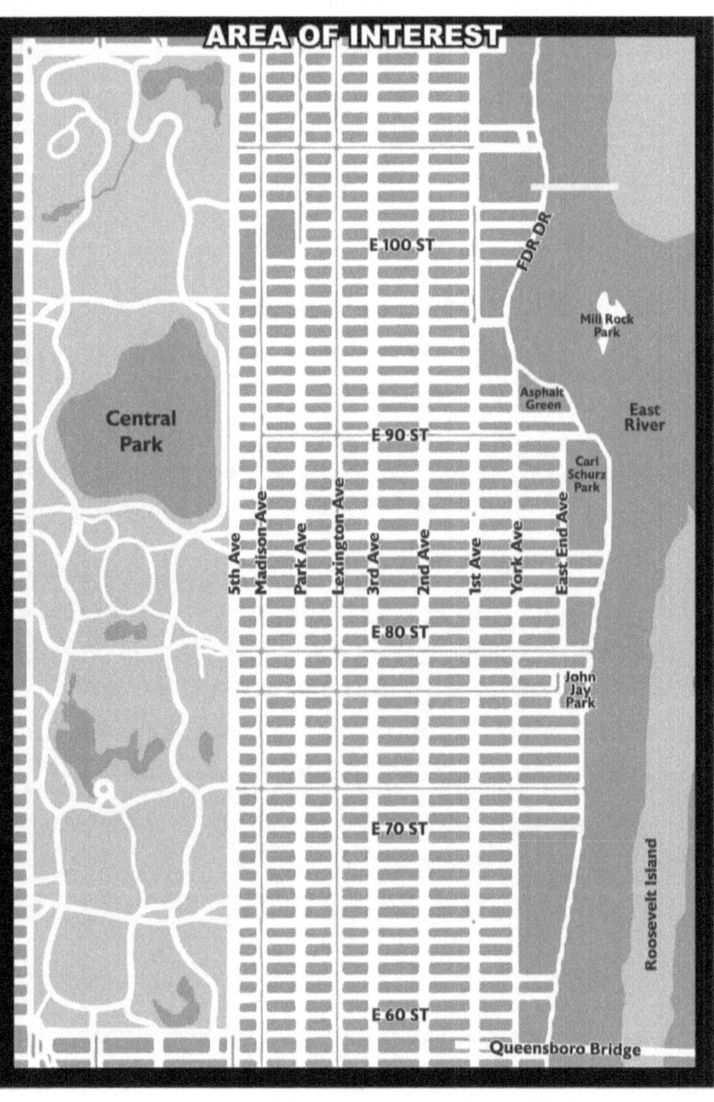

AREA OF INTEREST
Central Park
E 100 ST
E 90 ST
E 80 ST
E 70 ST
E 60 ST
5th Ave
Madison Ave
Park Ave
Lexington Ave
3rd Ave
2nd Ave
1st Ave
York Ave
East End Ave
FDR DR
Mill Rock Park
Asphalt Green
Carl Schurz Park
East River
John Jay Park
Roosevelt Island
Queensboro Bridge

"Nothing on earth consumes a man more quickly than
the passion of resentment."

~Friedrich Nietzsche

Prologue

Tommy had been assigned to the 5-3 squad in the Bronx for about a year and a half when he caught a particularly brutal homicide.

A young woman's body had been found stabbed to death and mutilated in the Mosholu Parkway Green. The killer had removed her left ear and left pinky finger and dragged her body under a thicket of bushes, a few feet off the intersection of Bainbridge Avenue and Mosholu Parkway.

Although the medical examiner's office had determined she had been dead for only approximately ten hours before her discovery, by some children walking to school, it was apparent that rats, or possibly even raccoons, had already eaten away part of her face and hands.

The woman had been stabbed eleven times in the neck, almost severing her head; twice in the chest, and once in the face. During a thorough search of the Green by the 5-3 squad and patrol officers, they found a large folding knife with a six-inch blade, which the forensics lab would later prove to be the murder weapon.

Additional evidence recovered at the scene included two sets of footprints in the soft loam beneath the shrubs that appeared to be related to the victim's location. Crime Scene techs made casts of the prints for future use. Samples of human hair and clothing fibers on the body that did not belong to her were also collected, and most damning of all were the skin samples under the fingernails.

Tommy and Detective Samuel Isaacs, Tommy's secondary in this investigation, had excellent forensic evidence attached to the case. Unfortunately, they didn't have any identification of their victim, a motive for the crime, or any idea as to where to start looking for the perpetrator of this brutally heinous act.

Six plus weeks into this investigation, Tommy sat at his desk in the 5-3, scratching notes onto a yellow pad.

He wrote down everything he knew about this case, which was very little, and everything he needed to know, which was a lot. He stared at photographs for hours and looked into dozens of past crimes and criminals with related similarities, but nothing, absolutely nothing, would pan out, no matter how many inquiries he made or doors he knocked on.

In the low hum of keyboards typing away as other members of the squad worked on their cases, Isaacs whooped out with a joyful burst of energy not befitting his fairly stoic personality.

"Bingo motherfuckers! Bing-Fucking-Go!"

The quiet of the room was broken, and the few detectives working in the squad room, eyes down and absorbed in their cases, all jumped in unison at Isaac's sudden outburst.

"Tommy, you handsome, lucky bastard!" Isaacs shouted, then relaxed his tone a bit and continued, "We got a person of interest in you're CUPPI," (Case or Circumstances Undetermined Pending Police Investigation) he said with a broad smile, something that was also rarely seen on the detective's face.

"Really? What do we have, Sam?" Tommy asked like a kid being handed a wrapped gift.

"An inquiry from a Detective Morse, from the Philadelphia PD to borough command. They have a suspect they are looking for, a, Yusef Jonstone. Fucker is wanted in connection to the murder of a 23-year-old hooker named Tanisha Gibbons, in the city of Philadelphia, approximately eighteen months ago."

"And you think they may be connected somehow?"

"Yes, I do… are you ready for this? – Victim was found stabbed twenty-two times under a highway overpass, knife wounds in her chest, head, and neck… She also had her left ear and left little finger amputated during the attack, how about that!"

"Alright! We got something, fuck me, we got more than something, we got a lead and a name, now we got to track this animal down, is there, -- do we got a photo?"

'Bzzt bzzt click click'– Isaacs pointed to the printer where that sound came from, "That's it, printing up right now."

"Fuck yeah!" Tommy said as he hopped up to look at the photo of that wrapped gift Issacs had just printed for him.

Tommy read aloud all the info they had just received on Yusef.

"Yusef Jonstone, aka Yusef Jones, aka John Yusef, aka Johnny Jones. Thirty-four years of age, the last known address is on North Howard Street, Philadelphia. The individual is also known to reside in Allentown, Pennsylvania, Washington, DC, Baltimore, Maryland, and Miami, Florida. According to this information, they are originally from Tampa, Florida. The attached rap sheet shows eighteen arrests, with at least one in each of the cities I just mentioned."

"Seems like this guy makes a move every time he gets in trouble?" Issacs interjected.

"Yeah, looks that way, don't it? A few robberies on here, shoplifting, a sexual assault in Miami, another in DC, promoting prostitution, in DC, our man has been busy."

Tommy and Isaacs immediately entered everything they had on Yusef Jonstone into their computers and could find nothing tying him to the Bronx or New York City. So, with a stack of photographs, they hit the streets for some old-school detective work and began canvassing the neighborhood.

The first stop was Jerome Avenue and 192nd Street, a common spot for street walkers to pick up Johns and service them in their cars, an alleyway, or the adjoining Saint James Park.

Tommy and Sam parked their car and approached a young lady working the corner of 192.

"Excuse me, dear, I need to ask you something," Tommy said.

"Whoa, you don't need to ask me nothin, honey. I'm just waiting for my ride to show up," the tall, thin, dark-skinned woman in a short black skirt, long red wig, and platform heels began. "I ain't out here workin' if that's what you thinkin', Mr. Police?"

"I don't care what you're doing, honey. I really don't. I just want to ask you a couple of questions, and then we'll leave you alone."

The woman looked him up and down with a bit of doubt in her eye.

"Well, go ahead then, I'm standing here."

"What's your name, dear?"

"They call me Raven." She replied with some contempt.

"I have a few photos I'd like to show you, Raven." Tommy showed her a photo of Yusef and continued, "Do you know, or have you ever seen this man?"

"Shit no, I don't know this nigga, what you lookin for him for?"

"Okay, I'm going to show you another photo. Tell me if you know this woman." He showed her a headshot of the still-unidentified victim.

"Aw, no, she dead… oh shit, she dead ain't she? And you two, you two is murder police, ain't y'all?"

"Yes, we're trying to find out who this girl and man are. We believe he is connected with her death, as we know he has killed working girls in the past, and we're afraid he is living somewhere here in the neighborhood."

"Let me see her again." Raven asked, "Motherfucker? He take her ear off?"

"Yes, he did."

"Okay, you know what. I'm gonna be real with y'all. I think I have seen her around here, but not for weeks, and this nappy-haired motherfucker, I ain't seen his ass, but you give me a card, I will call you if I sees him, I promise you that."

"So, you have seen her, do you know her name?"

"No, but I think she was from upstate, like Albany way, how she landed here, I got no idea."

Tommy talked a bit more with Raven and gave her his card. She again promised to call him if she saw the man they were looking for.

The detectives got back in their car, and as they started to drive away, Tommy spotted a short Puerto Rican woman walking out of the park. She wore a mini black and yellow striped skirt, high boots, and a pleather motorcycle jacket. He recognized her from when he was on patrol in the 5-3 several years prior. He pulled a U-turn and came alongside her as she walked down the sidewalk.

"Jazzy!" Tommy yelled out the car window. The woman stopped and squinted as she looked to see who was calling to her.

"You know me?" she asked as she approached. Time had taken a toll on her. Twenty-eight-year-old Jasmine Rodriguez had been working Jerome Avenue for the last twelve years, and those years had been less than kind to her.

"Tommy the cop!" she said with a big smile, showing a missing front tooth. "Oh man, oh man, I haven't seen you in forever! How you doing, man?" she asked with the sincerity of an old friend.

"Doing all right, Jazzy, how are you, honey?"

"Ehh, you know, getting by I guess, so what brings you round here man?" she asked, still standing on the curb.

Keane exited his vehicle and stepped up on the sidewalk with her, "A dead girl." He replied in a softer voice.

"Ahh, I don't want to hear that man."

"Here, please, I want you to look at a couple of photos."

"Of course, what you got?"

He showed her the picture of his Jane Doe, "Have you seen her?"

"Yup, yes sir, oh man, that's bad. She go by Bucky, because of her teeth, but her real name is Janeese, she an upstate girl."

"Last name?"

"Nah."

"You know anything else about her?"

"Not a lot. She showed up maybe like a year ago, crackhead, you know? She worked Jerome and the park, and the parking garage, nice girl, just lost with the drugs, you know? No tolerance, I mean you know, anything for the next hit, real risky behavior, even for us risk takers, you know?"

"Okay, how about this one?" Tommy asked as he held out the photo of Yusef Jonstone.

Jazzy stared silently at the photo, then, without taking her eyes off it, said, "He calls himself Johnny, and I don't like him. He got an evil vibe, he do this to Bucky?"

"We think so, this is who we're looking for, what can you tell me?"

"He been hangin' round here for a solid six months, nasty motherfucker, robbin people doing their shopping on Fordham Road, I think he stay on 184 by Grand Avenue somewhere, the mens calls him Philly."

"Does he still look like this? What does he usually wear?"

"His hair a little longer now, not quite dreads but kinda close, bunches it up in a scrunchie like a short ponytail on the top of his head, Nikes on his feet, black hoodie usually."

"Jazzy, it's so good to see you, kid. Thanks for the info," Tommy said as he put a $20 bill wrapped around his card in her hand and held it tightly with both of his for a moment.

"You too, Tommy, you be careful on these mean streets, motherfucker, I hate to hear anything bad happens to you! And if I see Johnny, I'll call you!"

"Please do, be careful and take care of yourself."

Tommy and Sam spent the rest of the night canvassing the area for Yusef. Thanks to Jazzy and Raven, their initial attempts at gaining information were fruitful, but the remainder of the night was a bust.

The next day, a computer search and a call to Albany positively identified Tommy's Jane Doe as Janeese Hotchkins, of Albany, New York.

Janeese had been arrested twice for possession and once for solicitation. Her last known address was at her grandmother's apartment, and though she had been in the Bronx for approximately fourteen months, no family member had ever reported her missing, which bothered Tommy quite a bit.

***

The following afternoon, at about 2:15 PM, Tommy's phone went off. "Keane," Tommy answered.

"Yo, Tommy, it's me, Jazzy, me and Raven here. We found your man Johnny, you know Philly, the guy you was lookin for last night. We followed him up Jerome from Fordham, and he in the McDonalds now. You know the one on Jerome over by the diner, he got his hair on top of his head like I said, black hoodie and Nikes on his feet. We gonna wait, but get here quick, if you can!"

"Oh, man! Thanks, Jazzy, I owe you big time. Be careful, kid; I'm on my way."

Tommy and Isaacs ran out of the precinct, hopped in their car, and drove as quickly as traffic would allow to the McDonald's on Jerome Avenue, pulling up just across the street.

As they exited the vehicle, Tommy saw Jazzy and Raven several car lengths away, nodding their heads yes and secretively motioning towards the restaurant.

As they crossed the avenue, Yusef stepped out the door and turned left, heading back toward Fordham Road. He saw the detectives as they approached. He certainly must have recognized them as police, but their casual manner and the fact that they didn't seem to notice him, or make eye contact, made him think they were simply going in for lunch just as he was leaving.

In a flash, Tommy rushed and grabbed Yusef from behind and immediately gave him a hip throw that took him off his feet, causing him to scream aloud before being planted face-first onto the concrete, with Tommy's knee digging deep into his back, pinning him down on the sidewalk. No sooner could Yusef begin to yell obscenities than Tommy had him cuffed.

The older white-haired Samuel Issacs leaned over at the waist and smiled at Yusef, who looked up at him with wide-open yellowing eyes, still not quite comprehending what had just happened, and said,

"Yusef, you filthy murdering bastard, you are under arrest, and we are going to send you away for a long, long time."

***

Yusef Jonstone was subsequently convicted of the murder of Janeese Hotchkins in the state of New York and received a twenty-year sentence. He was also convicted of the murder of Tanisha Gibbons by a jury in Philadelphia, Pennsylvania. He received a twenty-seven-year sentence, and two years later, he was charged and found guilty of the murder of Marcy DuPhrane by a jury in Miami, Florida.

It is believed he may have been responsible for two more homicides in the DC area; however, as of yet, he has not been charged in either.

***

About a week after Tommy arrested Yusef, Tommy and Sam picked up Jazzy and Raven from their usual spots on Jerome Avenue near 192nd Street and took them to the New Capital diner across the street and up the block from where the arrest was made.

They all sat at a table and had a meal together and had a good laugh.

The waitress, Virginia, and counterman Nick wondered what the story was with this strange quartet, who were obviously having a fun time.

When they finished eating, they thanked the ladies again for their help and gave each of them a fifty-dollar bill in appreciation.

Both Tommy and Sam understood kindness and respect. They knew that women like Jazzy and Raven received little of either in their lives, and therefore, showing their appreciation for the help they had given was much more important than just saying thank you.

Chapter One

Tommy's eye's opened to the sound of a car horn blowing and a man's voice cursing at someone else from the street below, "Move your ass!" the man yelled.

He rolled over and looked at Molly, who lay sleeping beside him. The dappled light made its way into the room through the laced curtains that hung over the windows.

He just stared at her for several minutes, taking in her loveliness. She faced him with the down comforter pulled up snugly to her neck, her beautiful green eyes closed. He studied her face, her long soft reddish eyelashes, the spattering of freckles across her nose and cheeks, her lips, jawline, and tiny ears, 'My god you are a beauty,' he thought to himself, 'What in the world do you see in me?'

It was the final few days of March, and Tommy had recovered entirely from the wounds he had received during the Li Jun case. His injuries and the situation that brought them on seemed to bother everyone around him more than they did him.

Molly, the beautiful young woman with whom he had just spent another night, had more than forgiven him for all but ignoring her throughout his four-week forced recovery.

Over the last couple weeks, he had been back at work in the 2-1 Squad and had put his life back into the order he was accustomed to. Granted, his life tended to be rather dangerous and chaotic, but for Tommy, it was the chaos, danger, and risk that came from being a New York City Police Detective that kept him motivated and got him out of bed every morning.

He puckered his lips and blew gently into Molly's face. he waited a moment and then did it a second time, this time getting a little reaction,

"Hey pretty face, you wanna get up?" he softly asked, "I got things to do before my tour tonight, but if you can get your lazy bones out of bed, we can grab breakfast before I go and do what I gotta do today."

"Mmmm," Molly hummed with a smile, her eyes still closed, "Blueberry pancakes?"

"Anything you want, sweet girl."

Her eyes opened, unaware that Tommy had been admiring her for the last several minutes,

"Blueberry pancakes, with too much butter, swimming in syrup."

"Okay, well then get your ass up, and let's get to it." He replied as he got up and headed towards Molly's bathroom to shower and brush his teeth.

"Can't we stay in bed for another hour? I'll make it worth your while?"

"No, come on now. If you want pancakes, you gotta move. I got important things I have to do this morning."

As Tommy began to lather himself up, eyes closed, the hot water beating down on his face, he felt the cooler hands of Molly on his chest as she stepped into the tub and wrapped herself around him,

"Well, since you're in a hurry, let's share this shower and save a little time, shall we?" she asked teasingly.

Her hands slowly explored Tommy's slick, soapy body, eventually finding their way to his quickly hardening erection,

"Oooh, are you keeping this extra clean for me? Can I, can I help you clean it?" she said softly as she gently stroked it repeatedly before Tommy turned to face her, lifting her off the tub floor, pinning her to the wall, and slowly entering her.

Molly gasped as it happened and put her arms around his neck, pulling herself in close for a kiss while wrapping her legs around his waist. Unhurried and rhythmically, he slid himself in and out of her until she came to a body-shaking climax, which forced Tommy to finish as well.

As they toweled one another off, he commented,

"Molly, you are by far one of the friskiest women I have ever met." Stealing another kiss.

"And you, Tommy, are by far one of the sexiest men I have ever met."

After getting dressed, they strolled to the Gracie Mews Diner on the corner of 81st and 1st to satisfy Molly's lust for blueberry pancakes. Afterwards, they returned to her building, and he kissed her again. He then went home to his mother's apartment on 88th, where he was greeted by his best friend, JoJo, the little black and white dog.

"Hey, Ma, how you doing? You ready for your appointment with Dr. Andrews?" he asked his mother Maria, who sat in her recliner, smoking a cigarette, watching television.

"Yes, yes, Tommy, I am. I'd like to walk today, Tommy. It's a lovely day, and I want to walk to his office today."

"Absolutely, it's not far, and it is nice out. I know March is almost over, but it feels more like a warm May morning. Does JoJo need to go out before we leave?

"No, Tommy, I just had him out. Bad boy did his business right in front of Holy Trinity again, Tommy."

"JoJo, you naughty boy, what's with you and that church?" He jokingly asked the little dog for his mother's benefit.

Together, they walked arm in arm down 2nd Avenue to 86th Street and then up to the medical office, which was on 86th between 5th and Madison Avenue. Maria beamed with pride the whole way during their walk. She loved her son and was extremely happy to have him back at home on a semi-regular basis ever since his transfer to the 21st Precinct.

Maria also liked Dr. Andrews. In general, she enjoyed most of her doctors. She held them all in esteem and strongly revered the medical profession. The way she saw it, a priest may help you when it came to heaven, but doctors helped you here on earth.

Dr. Andrews was Maria's neurologist and had been seeing her for the last twenty-eight months. He was the one who had diagnosed her with Alzheimer's, and this would now be her 8th visit.

Every test that could be run had been run, and Dr. Andrews had fully explained that this was indeed what they had feared it was, well over two years before. However, he still kept appointments with her to track her progression and help her with medications as things continued to deteriorate.

Tommy described how his mother was still sharp, although increasingly quirky, and how she managed her days quite well. She could get around the neighborhood on her own with no problems, make and show up to all her appointments on her own, and, in general, still lead a normal life.

Maria agreed and stated that "I've never felt better." This, of course, was an exaggeration, as Dr. Andrews and Tommy could note the decline in her speech, although she passed the brief memory exam with 100% correct answers to the eight questions she had been asked.

Dr. Andrews also showed them how her last scan had shown a slight decrease in brain mass, basically confirming that, outside of some surprise illness or event, Alzheimer's was going to be how Maria would meet her end. It was just a matter of how long it would take.

The only positive thing the doctor had to say was that this awful disease affected every victim differently. Some people could live with it for years or even decades, while others could pass within months. Many kept their faculties about them through most of their illness. In contrast, others could completely lose their minds and be totally lost to the world, but so far, twenty-eight months into her diagnosis, she appeared to be doing quite well, "As well as can be expected, and better than most," is how Dr. Andrews put it.

Tommy and Maria Keane, then again, arm in arm, made their way back to their apartment on 88th, Maria no worse for wear after they met with Dr. Andrews.

Much like her son, Maria had a way of accepting things for what they were. She never dwelled or ruminated on anything negative; sure, she could get angry or sad over life events, but once things were done, they were done. The fact that she had Alzheimer's disease and would most likely die from it within the next few years or less, to Maria, was simply the way it was. She had been dealt this hand and would play it out till the end, happy to be in the game as long as possible.

***

Tommy walked into the 2-1 station house about fifteen minutes before his shift. He nodded to Sgt Ruffalo behind the desk and gave a wink to Officer Ortiz, who sat at the TS (telephone/switchboard), then made his way up to the squad room on the second floor.

As he stepped in, he exclaimed, "What the fuck is with this building! It's almost seventy degrees outside, and the heat is still cranking in here. It's bad enough how warm they keep it during the winter, but for Christ's sake, turn it off and save a few dollars, will ya!"

Detective Keogh stood up from his desk. He was about six feet six and close to three hundred pounds. He raised his hands up high, showing the giant circles of sweat under his arms,

"I'm dying here, Tommy, these fuckers are going to kill me, it's intentional, I swear they want me dead before I make retirement."

Keogh's partner Volpe laughed, "And look at this little guinea fuck," Keogh continued, "He's loving it, makes him feel like he's back in old Napoli!"

"What can I say, my people do good in the heat, unlike you Irish barbarians running around that cold, rainy, shitty little island you call a nation in skirts."

Tommy hung his coat up, wondering why he bothered to bring it. He then took his sports jacket off, as he was already beginning to sweat in the unbearable office temperature. He took a seat at an empty desk and began his day with a new domestic violence case folder he had yet to address from the week before.

As Keogh, Volpe, and the rest of the A team signed out for the day, Tommy and Doreen were the only two people in the squad room, with Sergeant Browne alone in his office.

Tommy stood up and complained again about the heat, as he grabbed himself a bottle of water. He then sat back down and rolled up his sleeves, in a weak attempt to get a little more relief. As he did, Doreen noticed a tattoo on his left forearm.

"What is that? A tattoo, Mr. Man? I didn't know you had a tattoo."

"Well, I'm sure there are many things you don't know about me, Doreen."

"Obviously. What is that exactly? It looks like a Claddagh from here."

"No, it's a set of paratrooper wings."

"Ahh, from when you were in the army."

"Yup," He answered, not paying attention to her, as he banged away on his keyboard.

"You got any more?"

"Yeah, a few."

"A few! How do I not know you have a few tattoos?"

"Well, I guess because you've never seen me without my clothes on?"

"So, what you got?"

"I have the wings you see," Tommy began, still not taking his eyes from his keyboard or pausing to look up at Doreen, "A rose with my sister Kathleen's name on my chest, a heart with my wife's name, Cookie, on my arm, an angel inside the same arm with my daughter Caitlyn's name, and another rose on my other arm with Mom, in the banner."

Tommy intentionally left out the banner on top of his shoulder that read 89th Street, over a faded shamrock, because he didn't want to get into a neighborhood conversation with Doreen. To this date, no one from the squad other than its newest arrival, Tommy's old friend Clay, knew he was originally from Yorkville, within the confines of the 2-1.

Tommy wanted to keep it that way, and he also wanted to make sure that this particular tattoo wasn't referenced to the same one his lifelong friend, and arch-criminal, Terry Calahan, wore on his shoulder. Two conversations he was hoping to avoid having with anyone in the precinct, even Doreen, whom he had grown truly fond of over the last six months they had worked together.

"Wow! I never knew, you're like a full-blown tattoo guy!"

"I don't know about that," Tommy replied, still trying to do his typing.

"Can I see them?"

"No."

"No? What do you mean, no?"

"I mean no. I'm not taking my shirt off to show you my tattoos."

"Come on! I'll show you mine if you show me yours."

"While that's tempting, the answer is still no, I'm not taking my shirt off, and I don't care about your tattoo either."

"You sure? You don't wanna see mine, it's pretty cute."

"Oh my god, if you show me, will you leave me alone and let me finish this form I'm typing?"

Doreen stood up and stepped around the desk. "Gee, you are no fun at all today." She said as she undid her belt and rolled her slacks down to just above her bikini line to reveal a cute little butterfly that was about the size of a quarter.

"Haha, and you call that a tattoo?" He laughed, and as he did, Lieutenant Bricks and Jimmy Colletti stepped into the Squad Room,

"Whoa ho! What is going on here?" Jimmy asked in an excited tone.

Lieutenant Bricks also smiled at the sight of his Detective, Doreen Doyle, standing in front of a seated Tommy Keane with her pants rolled halfway down to her crotch, "Yes, what do we have here?" He asked.

"Oh, nothing you perverts, I'm just showing Tommy my tattoo, that's all," Doreen replied, and she pulled her slacks back up and buckled her belt, her face flushing with embarrassment at literally being caught with her pants down. "Turns out Tommy is loaded with them, and he wanted to see mine?"

"Wanted?" Tommy asked.

"Alright, whatever you kids do while you're alone is your business, I guess? But what say we try to keep our pants on while we're in the office," Said Lieutenant Bricks, not letting the joke die. "Also, on an entirely different note, we have some special news today. Jim, you want to tell them?"

"Sure, Lu, thanks," then looking to Doreen and Tommy, "I made the sergeant's list, crushed the test, and will be going into the next class."

"Congratulations!" Doreen shouted and hopped to her feet to give him a big hug.

"You're leaving us, Jimmy?" Tommy asked in a more somber tone.

"Yes sir, not for a few weeks, but yeah, it looks that way," Jimmy replied with a huge grin.

Tommy smiled back, but it was a rather insincere smile. Like he had with Doreen, Tommy was becoming fond of Jimmy and thought he wanted to be a detective, sure he currently was a detective. Still, Tommy thought Jimmy wanted to become a true detective, a seasoned investigator, and believed he had what it took to not only do the job but to do it well.

There were many different avenues one's career could take in the NYPD, and literally hundreds of various jobs were within the department, and there was no doubt that Patrol, as they said, was the department's backbone.

The men and women in uniform who responded to call after call, were first on the scene and who took report after report from the simplest things like a noise complaint, to the most horrific of homicides.

However, for Tommy, the investigators, the detectives of the Detective Bureau, and particularly the Precinct Squad Detectives, were the true backbone. They were the people who went after and hunted down society's worst. They took on the many faces of evil, case by case, and were able to make the biggest contributions to the safety of the city's residents and give what little, if any, consolation to the victims of the savage criminals that terrorized their streets.

With these beliefs in mind, Tommy was a little disappointed to hear that his new friend, the young detective Jimmy Colletti, would soon be leaving the 2-1 Squad and turning in his Detective shield for a Sergeant's shield and some stripes.

- 24 -

Chapter Two

Day One:

Mark, Clay, and Jimmy had left the heat of the Squad Room to go out and do some interviews, leaving Tommy and Doreen to attend to different unsolved cases and paperwork they both needed to complete.

"Who's catching today?" Sergeant Browne yelled from his desk inside his cramped office, the door open to the squad room more so he could listen, then be heard.

"Tommy is today, Boss!" Detective Doyle yelled back.

"Is he not in at the moment?"

"He is, not sure where, either the locker room or the little boy's room?"

"Okay, well, grab him, you got a body, a young dead woman over at 407 East 82nd, 4th floor, patrol is on the scene, they say she was shot with an arrow?"

"An arrow?" Doreen said, "Okay, Boss, we'll get on it." She shouted back and began to gather her things and put on her jacket, just as Tommy stepped into the office.

"Grab your jacket there Mr. Man, you got a young woman to attend to."

"What's that?" he asked.

"You got a body, a woman on 82nd, Browne says she was killed with an arrow? Or at least has an arrow in her?"

"An arrow? That's a first for me."

***

8:16PM
407 East 82nd Street.

Tommy and Doreen stopped at the corner and waited for the officer on post to lift the police tape so their vehicle could fit underneath. They drove down the block and parked in front of Saint Steven's of Hungary Catholic School, which was directly across the street from the address where the body was discovered.

Both detectives exited the vehicle and quickly scanned the block. They noticed the head of what appeared to be a woman, sitting in the back seat of one of the patrol cars, a uniformed officer in front of her in the driver's seat.

It was obvious which building they were headed to as they could see Officers McCartney and Rios talking on the stoop opposite the parked patrol cars.

"Upstairs, 4th floor," Officer McCartney stated in a serious tone as Tommy and Doreen approached, "Sergeant Diaz is up there waiting on you."

"Thanks." Doreen softly replied as the two entered the building and began to climb the stairs of the old four-story walk-up tenement. The only sounds were the officer's radios keying on and off echoing down from the floors above, bouncing off the hard plaster walls and tiled floors as they approached the crime scene.

"Detectives Keane and Doyle, how you two doing this evening?" Sergeant Diaz asked as he heard them walk up the last flight and turned to greet them.

"Good, Diaz, how you makin' out?" asked Tommy.

Doreen said, "Good Sarge, you?"

She looked through the railing's balusters, eye level with a young woman's body, who lay facing straight up toward the ceiling. The girl's big, blue, eyes were open wide, as if still in shock, with an arrow stuck in her throat. A pool of blood surrounded her head and neck, oozing itself in and under a full head of long blonde hair.

"I was doing alright until we got called over here for this awful mess, definitely not the way I was hoping to spend my tour or start my week."

"Hmm, we're right there with you, pal, what do we know?" Tommy asked.

"Nothing really. A neighbor lady came home, found this, and ran out of the building as she called 911 on her cell. We have her in a car downstairs, she didn't have much to say to the responding officers or when I arrived. I instructed everyone not to ask her anything until you arrived."

"Who was first on scene?"

"Rios and McCartney."

"Again? I'm gonna start calling them the 'First on Scene Twins,' if they keep this up."

Sergeant Diaz cocked his head, not quite understanding what Tommy was getting at.

"They were first on the scene when that Chinese girl was tossed out the window a couple of months ago," Tommy said to clarify, as he could see Diaz's confusion.

"Oh yeah right, fuck that was an awful scene," Sergeant Diaz replied.

"Ain't they all?" Tommy said as he squatted down next to the body in the narrow corridor between apartments, taking his first close look at this poor young woman's corpse. "We have a name?"

"Yes, Heather Mills," Sergeant Diaz replied, "But that's all we got. The neighbor lady was pretty distraught when we arrived. Hopefully, we'll have more once she calms down, and you can interview her. Heather Mills lives in apartment 4FW, and the neighbor is there in 4RW." He pointed down the hallway.

"Okay, so this is going to be a bit of a cluster fuck of a crime scene," Tommy began, "We can have no one coming in or out until the Crime Scene Unit gives us the go ahead. We may have evidence on anyone of these floors and staircases leading up to here, same with the stoop. We can't afford to have anyone smudging a print on any handrails, or adding more samples anywhere along the way… Do us a favor, Doreen, please go downstairs and have McCartney and Rios tape off everything around the building. Keep everyone off the stoop and on the sidewalk in front of the building… And hey, hands in pockets for anyone entering or leaving the premises."

"You got it, Tommy," Doreen replied.

"And fuck me, you got someone else we could use, Sarge? This is the fourth floor; I'd like someone assigned to monitor the halls and steps to make sure we keep folks in their apartments until Crime Scene arrives and does their thing."

"Absolutely," replied Sergeant Diaz, and both he and Doreen headed down the stairs.

Tommy remained squatting over the corpse and began to study his victim and her surroundings. Heather Mills was an exceptionally attractive woman with large blue eyes, well-kept long blonde hair, nicely applied makeup, and nails. She was dressed in tight jeans, high boots, and an expensive-looking waist-length lambskin jacket with a faux fur collar. Still wearing gold earrings, chains, rings, and what appeared to be an unopened purse still at her side, Tommy immediately removed robbery as a motive for this crime.

As he continued to take in the scene, Doreen made it back up the stairs, and they both stood next to one another, staring down at the body.

"Damn, she's a good-looking girl," Doreen said, "I bet we're going to find out she's a model or an actress, no one looks this beautiful and doesn't get paid for it."

"I'm going to agree with you there." Tommy replied, "Poor thing, who would do this to you?"

Tommy notified Sergeant Browne and Lieutenant Bricks of what they found at the scene, and a few minutes later,

Detectives Mark Stein, Clay Johnson, and Jimmy Colletti joined Tommy and Doreen and aided in the preliminary investigation.

Crime Scene arrived and did their business. They photographed the entire interior of the building's hallways, stairways, and landings and dusted every surface from the front stoop to the roof's landing in search of prints.

Medical Examiner Kristin Smyth appeared on the scene and concluded that Miss Mills was indeed dead. The cause of death was most likely the arrow that was lodged in her throat, and she asked that Tommy call her the following day for a time to come in for the autopsy.

As soon as Crime Scene and ME Smyth were through, Tommy and Doreen gave Heather Mills' body a thorough search.

They recovered the keys to her apartment from her jacket pocket, her identification, credit cards, gym membership, different pieces of makeup, a small cigarette box containing two joints, and a little baggie with three little blue pills with SKY imprinted on them.

Tommy then took Heather's keys and tried each one until he could open the door to her apartment. Drawing his .9mm Smith and Wesson from its holster, he looked back at Doreen,

"Be cool, don't touch anything. This may end up being part of our crime scene, and we don't want to disturb anything. And if we decide we do want to disturb something, you know we're going to have to wait for a warrant anyway to really dig into this place."

Doreen nodded in agreement as she drew her .9mm Glock, and Tommy opened the door to Heather Mills' studio apartment.

"Police!" he shouted, "Anyone in here? Police 21st Precinct NYPD! Let us know you're here!"

The apartment was a nicely renovated, a relatively sizeable one-room studio. Two windows faced the street, and a small kitchenette was at the rear with a decent-sized bathroom behind it. The place was clean, well-appointed, and quite stylish. There would have been nothing at all to raise the detective's interest except for the camera, which sat on a tripod in front of a queen-size brass bed. Behind the camera were two round 18-inch ring lights on tripods facing the bed.

Tommy and Doreen looked at one another and then back at the camera/lighting set up. Neither said a word, although Doreen raised one eyebrow.

At the moment, they had no idea what the story was with this scene, and it felt disrespectful to begin to judge this young woman while her body was still being put into a bag by the Medical Examiner's techs in the hallway just feet from where they stood.

The cursory search of the apartment yielded nothing of value, so the detectives left the studio, locked the door, and placed a neon green police crime scene seal on the door and jam, forbidding entrance.

They started down the stairs, passing the Crime Scene investigators who were still lifting prints on the lower floors. They walked outside to Sergeant Diaz's car, where they met with Heather's neighbor, Irene Fisk.

Ms. Fisk had calmed down quite a bit since her original meeting with Officers McCartney and Rios. It was visible she had been crying, as the little line of eyeliner she wore was smudged from wiping her tears. Irene was a short, round, brunette of sixty, dressed in loose-fitting light blue pants and an oversized navy cardigan. She was able to answer the detective's questions without hesitation, calmly, and with excellent acuity.

"How well did you know Miss Mills?" Tommy asked.

"I like to say fairly well. She moved into the building about two and a half years ago; we see each other in passing a couple of times a week; she's a genuinely courteous young woman."

"Did you talk often?"

"Yes, most every time we meet, we'd chat for a minute or two, and on occasion, we'd go to the laundromat together. A few times this year, we have gone out for coffee. I'd say we are…" Irene paused as the reality of the situation hit her. She took a swallow and a breath to calm herself. "I'd say we were casual friends."

"Can you tell us what she did for a living?" Doreen asked.

"She came to New York from Ohio to be an actress. She, as you can see, was a beautiful girl; she could also sing and dance, but she couldn't find work in that field. She's had several jobs over the last few years, but for the last year or so, she has been making a good deal of money with" Irene paused for a moment, and she lowered her voice, wanting to save Heather Mills somehow some shame or embarrassment, "on An Only-Fans site."

"Only-Fans?" Tommy questioned.

"It's an online porn site," Doreen replied, "Girls, and I assume some guys, strip and perform sexual acts on webcams for their fans who have paid subscriptions."

Tommy nodded, which answered the question about the camera and lights.

"Did she," Tommy paused, "Did Miss Mills ever entertain guests here in her apartment?"

"No, if you're asking if she was a hooker, no, she… Heather was a polite and decent person. She worked hard trying to do the acting thing, but needed to make money. She's paying over three thousand a month for that tiny studio, and well… What can I say, I'm pretty anti-porn, but she found a way to make some money. More money than she could as a waitress or barista, and on her own terms, right here at home. It freed her up for auditions and call-backs for her acting career in a way that no other job could."

"Is there a boyfriend?"

"There have been a couple; the first one was a boy, a man, I'm sorry, these people are so young, a young man named Dave. He moved to London for business, which broke her heart. They were still in contact, but long-distance relationships never work. There is, was, a new guy, Logan, Logan Mathews, I think, he seemed nice, he was a model, very handsome, not very bright."

"You say was, so they broke up?"

"Yes, because of the webcamming. He demanded she stop, and she wouldn't, she didn't care enough about Logan to stop it for him, I bet she would have stopped it for Dave though…"

"Do you think…" Tommy began to ask but was interrupted by Irene.

"Think Logan did this? I can't see it; don't think he would have it in him. He is a tall, well-built, young man, but I don't think he would have the stones for something like this, to be honest. Obviously, I could be wrong, but he, well, Logan just doesn't seem hard enough to take part in such a brutal act."

"You wouldn't happen to have Logan's contact information, do you, or Heather's parents, or family information?"

"No, I'm sorry. I don't believe I have anything; I don't know if I have much more to share at all, to tell you the truth. I liked Heather. I think she had a lot to offer the world, but sadly, I think she was a little misguided in how to lead her life. I hope you don't judge her poorly for the webcams. She was just a young girl desperate for money and a career, and young women these days, well, I don't think they often realize the future ramifications of their actions."

"Ms. Fisk, I could not agree with you more about that, and no, no, we would never judge anyone on what they do with their lives as long as they're not hurting others."

Tommy handed Irene Fisk a card.

"Here is my card. Please let me know if you think of anything, no matter how small. I'll likely contact you again soon about today's events. Thank you so much for your time, and I'm very sorry for your loss."

It took almost two more hours before all aspects of Tommy's preliminary on-scene investigations concluded, and he returned to the squad room. Jimmy Colletti and Clay Johnson informed him that there were a few bits of videotape from nearby businesses and building security cameras to review.

Mark Stein had found Logan Mathews's address, ran him through the department system, and discovered no prior arrests.

Doreen had done a thorough social media search and found quite a bit on several of his pages; he seemed to spend hours a day attempting to become an influencer. Most of it was fairly vapid nonsense, but she did find three highly unflattering posts in which he called out Heather Mills by name.

"My X-Heather, the filthy camwhore, should rot in hell."

"Fucking Heather, what's next? Hardcore gangbangs? I hope they fuck her to death, fucking whore!"

And probably the most damning.

"Fucking cunt bitch Heather whore, yes, I'm embarrassed, and if I have an STD she's going to pay, I will end that bitch! Fuck her, I may end her either way!"

- 36 -

Chapter Three

01:23 AM

25-93 38th Street, Astoria, Queens, NY, apartment of Logan Mathews.

Tommy, Doreen, Clay, and Jimmy parked in front of 25-93 38th Street in the dead quiet neighborhood of Astoria, across the bridge in Queens County.

Tommy and Clay went to the front of Logan's apartment. Doreen and Jimmy posted themselves outside at either corner of the small, multifamily home in case their suspect decided to attempt an escape via a window.

Tommy knocked on the door and rang the bell, waited a few seconds, and again knocked and rang the bell.

"Okay, just a minute," a man's voice came from behind the door, then again, "Who is it?"

"We're from Con Edison, the gas company. There's a report of a gas leak; we need to check all the apartments in the building."

The locks on the door began to tumble, and a tall, young, handsome man wearing sweatpants and a snug-fitting T-shirt opened the door. It was Logan Mathews.

Logan immediately cocked his head to the side, realizing the two men standing in front of him were most definitely not Con Ed workers. Seeing the detective shield Clay was holding in his hand and both men's hands gripping their holstered pistols, he stepped back and stuttered as his eyes opened wider.

"Wah, wah- what's going on here? Ya-you two aren't from the gas company!"

"No, we are not. We are detectives from the 21st precinct, and you are coming with us, Logan. We have some questions we want to ask you." Tommy said flatly.

"I don't think I'm going anywhere with you!" Logan said as his eyes widened, and his heart began to pound faster.

"Oh, I beg to differ, young man," Clay replied.

"Do you have a warrant?" Logan asked.

"Nope, don't need one. You are a person of interest to us, and you will return to the 21st precinct with us for questioning. I know it's quite early in the morning, or late at night, depending on how you look at it, but this is one of those no-choice kind of things. So please, don't make this hard for us, because I promise we can make it so much harder on you," Tommy replied, stepping inside the doorway.

"Am I under arrest? For what? What did I do?"

"We're not charging you with anything at the moment, Logan, but we're going to have a long talk about where you were tonight and your relationship with Heather Mills."

"Heather, who? I've been here all night, all night, you can ask my girlfriend, she's in the bedroom. Go ahead and ask her; she'll tell you, I've been right here all night."

"Step outside," Tommy said calmly. "Turn around," he cuffed Logan. "What's your girl's name?"

"Jen." Logan answered, a tear running down his cheek.

"You got him, Clay? I'm going to check on his girl."

Clay responded, "Sure do."

Tommy stepped inside the apartment, through the kitchen area, and knocked on what appeared to be the bedroom door.

"Jen, you in there? This is the police." He said loudly and firmly, as his hand drew his .9mm Smith and Wesson halfway out of its holster.

"Yes," a woman's voice answered, "I'm in here, what's wrong?" she said as she slowly opened the door.

A young, nice -looking woman in her mid-twenties, Jen stood in the doorway, wearing a black T-shirt and tight jeans that were yet to be buttoned and zipped up. She had just yanked them on while she overheard part of the conversation happening in the living room.

"Hello, dear. We are going to take Logan in for some questioning. I'm sorry to frighten you, I just wanted you to know what was happening."

"Uh, uh okay, I'm not frightened, just a little confused. What is happening? I mean, I don't understand. What has he done?"

"I'm not at liberty to discuss that now, Jen… what's your last name?"

"Arcola. What the fuck man? What is happening?"

"Do you live here, Jen?"

"No, sir."

"Can I ask you how long you and Logan have been together?"

"This is like only our third date."

"And how long have you been together tonight, this evening, in particular?"

"I don't know. I left work at 11:00 and came right over, so maybe the last two hours?"

"Really? Okay, dear, I'm sorry to do this to you, but you're going to come with us, alright? We're going to take you to the 21st precinct in Manhattan. We're going to ask you a few questions, okay, I want you to know you are absolutely not in trouble, do you understand that? We must talk to you and Logan and get some facts straight."

"Oh my god! Really? Holy shit, what's going on officer? You're scaring me."

"You have nothing to fear, Jen, I promise you. You're not in trouble, we just have some questions, and we'll get you out of there as quickly as possible."

As Jen got dressed, Tommy grabbed a hooded sweatshirt from the back of a chair and a pair of Logan's sneakers and gave them to Clay for Logan to put on. Clay took Logan and sat him in the back seat of Tommy's car, then walked Jen Arcola to Clay and Jimmy's car and removed both to the 2-1 Precinct.

***

2:55 AM

21st Precinct Interview Room, The Box.

Tommy sat at the table across from Logan in the interview room, holding a yellow pad and pen.

Doreen, Mark, and Clay stood in the observation room while Jimmy sat with Jen Arcola in the Muster room across the hall from the Squad Room to ensure she and Logan had no verbal or visual contact.

"Alright, Logan, I know you have some questions, but we're gonna take this slow, okay? I have several questions, so please just answer them. When I'm done, you can ask me anything you like. The only thing I will request from you before we get started is for you to tell me the truth. You won't be doing yourself any favors by lying to me. Do you understand?"

"What the fuck is going on here man, you pull me out of bed in the middle of the…"

"Oh! Slow down, Logan. Remember what I just said? You can ask me whatever you want; just let me ask you what I need to, okay?"

Logan, visibly annoyed, nodded his head yes.

"Alright, simple one, where were you tonight between 7:00 and 8:00 PM?"

"Home."

"Okay then, at home." Tommy made a note on his yellow pad, "What time did you get there, and what were you doing before you got home?"

"I had a couple of modeling go-sees in the city."

"Go-sees? Forgive me, please explain."

"It's an audition, you go and see if they want you for the job."

"Ahh, got you, is that what you do for work then? You're a professional model?"

"Yes, I model and act."

"And that's how you pay your bills?"

"I'm also a server at a restaurant, you know… to help make ends meet."

"Okay, so you wait tables to pay the bills, and then do some modeling and acting jobs when you can, cool, got it… So, you were in the city today, what time did you get back to Astoria then?"

"I don't know about six I think, but really not sure."

"Is there any way to confirm you were back in Queens at that time?"

"Well, yeah, if you asked my girl Jen at the apartment, she would have told you."

"Yeah, well, unfortunately, we needed to bring you in here for this. Nice looking girl, that Jen, how long have the two of you been dating?"

"Not long, just a few weeks."

"But you guys are close, like boyfriend-girlfriend?"

"Oh yeah, definitely." He nodded his head.

"And you and Jen have been together since 6:00 PM this evening?"

"Yeah, well, give or take. Again, I'm not sure exactly; I've never really been good at keeping track of time."

"Okay, but we can say, in general, since you got home, is that fair to say? And you two spent the entirety of the evening together in your apartment there in Astoria, you and your girlfriend Jen, yes?"

"Yes, correct."

"Excuse me for just a minute, I need to take a piss and grab something to drink. Can I get you anything while I'm up? A coffee, water, soda?"

"I'll take a water."

Tommy got up and headed over to the observation room. Clay opened the door, and he, Mark, and Doreen stepped into the hallway.

"Alright. So, we got him in the city today, other than that I'm not buying what this kid is selling, what do you two think so far?"

"He's full of it," Doreen replied.

"I don't know if he's our man yet, but he ain't being honest, that's for sure," said Clay.

"He's nervous and he's not telling the truth," Was Mark's take.

"Clay, Mark, keep an eye on this guy. Doreen, come with me. We'll ask our girl Jen a couple of questions. I'd like you there for the feminine touch if it's needed."

Tommy and Doreen went to the muster room, where Jen sat on a plastic chair, her head leaning back against the wall, staring up at the ceiling, and her left leg nervously bouncing up and down.

"Sorry to have kept you waiting, Jen, but this may take a while. Let me ask you again, and please try to be as exact as possible… What time did you and Logan get together tonight?"

"Like I told you before, about 11:20, maybe 11:30?"

"And how long have you been seeing him?"

"Seeing him? Well, we've just hooked up, you know, gotten together three times, including tonight, tonight would be the third time we've met up."

"Okay, so, just to clarify: you two aren't boyfriend and girlfriend then?"

Jen pursed her lips and shook her head, "No, not hardly, I mean definitely not, we met at a bar the weekend before last, and we've seen each other three times, including tonight, he's never even taken me out to dinner."

"Okay, have you guys had any, many deep conversations? Do you talk a lot when you get together?"

Jen looked at Tommy as if he didn't understand anything.

"Not really, I mean yeah we talk about stuff, but mostly just have a couple drinks, smoke some weed, and have sex, you know, we just hook up for a few hours, and that's it."

"Alright, what have you talked about then?"

"You know, typical shit, relationships, music, not a lot, to tell you the truth. Really, I just like him cause he's so damn good-looking."

Doreen nodded and raised her eyebrows in agreement, which seemed to put Jen a little more at ease.

"Has he ever spoken about any of his past girlfriends, Jen?" Doreen then asked.

"Just one, some actress from here in the city. The first night we met, he went on about what a bitch she was, and that he had to get tested for an STD because he couldn't trust her, said she was a porn star."

"Her name?" Doreen asked.

"Oh, I don't know, I can't remember."

"Heather?" Tommy asked.

"Yeah, that's it…" Jen paused, "That means something, doesn't it?" She said with a concerned look and lilt to her voice.

"Yes, we found Heather dead at about 8:00 PM tonight."

"Oh, my fuckin god! Was it, do you think it was… Holy shit!" Jen exclaimed, and her knee began to bounce again.

"We don't know, that's what we're trying to find out. Can you tell us anything more about Logan?" Doreen asked.

"Oh, my fuckin god! No, no, not really."

"Logan told me you were his girlfriend, and you two have been dating for a few weeks now, and that you got together at about 6:00 PM tonight, once he returned from some modeling go-sees here in the city earlier today," Tommy explained.

"No!" She replied excitedly, "That's not true, none of that is fuckin true. I was at work until eleven and have only been with him… Oh my fuckin god, I have been with him … I've been to his apartment three times, that's it, I swear on my mother's grave. Three times, that's it, and what, last weekend, the weekend before, and tonight, and that's it, I mean, fuck, I don't even know his last name."

Tommy and Doreen left Jen with Jimmy in the muster room. Her head was bowed, resting in her hands, and her leg bouncing with nerves.

Tommy joined Logan in the box again, while Doreen rejoined Clay and Mark in the observation room.

He took his seat across from Logan and set a bottle of water in front of him,

"Sorry for the delay, I had to run downstairs for the water. We were out up here."

"No problem," Logan replied, opening the bottle and taking a big swig.

Tommy paused momentarily, thinking about how he would proceed with his questioning. He had Logan in the city today, and if he was indeed back in Queens by 6:00 PM, why would he lie about it and pull Jen Arcola into the mix? And the social media posts? He threatened her via social media and thought telling Jen Arcola that he hated Heather Mills was necessary. Telling a young woman he hardly knew, and a possible romantic interest, about how you hated your ex-porn star girlfriend seemed a little odd, and a little obsessive. So far, Logan was coming off as the textbook bitter ex-boyfriend.

"When was the last time you saw Heather, Logan?"

Logan physically tightened up and paused for a moment, as if he were thinking about the right answer.

"Heather, who? I, I know a few Heathers."

Tommy leaned back in his chair and looked intently into Logan's eyes, pausing and sighing in disbelief. Any sense of warmth or friendliness had left Tommy's body, and a palpable cold disdain now instantly filled the room.

"Which Heather do you think I'm asking you about?"

Logan's face paled as he struggled to answer, "I, I, uhm, I don't, I'm not sure, Detective, I guess, maybe you're asking me about my ex-girlfriend, Heather Mills?"

"When was the last time you saw Heather, Logan?" Tommy asked again, even more intently.

Logan nervously answered, "I, I, I, don't know, Detective, I don't know why you're asking me this. I haven't seen or been anywhere near her in weeks… Not for weeks, I, I swear, and I definitely haven't seen her today, is that where we're going here? Is that what you want to know?"

"How long have you two been broken up?"

"A, just a few weeks, I'm not sure, three maybe five or more?"

"Why did you break up?"

"I, we just, well…" Logan paused, "We just wanted to see other people, you know, we're both young, and neither of us enjoyed being tied down, you, you know how it goes."

"Actually, no, I don't. Seems like Heather was quite a beautiful young woman, something a fella would want to hold onto."

"Yeah, well, looks aren't everything, and besides, she was the one who really wanted to end it, yeah, she chose to break it off, not me."

"Did that make you angry? I imagine a handsome professional model like yourself isn't used to rejection?"

"Hey, she didn't reject me, alright, we had a good thing going for a while, she just, oh man…" Logan paused for a moment, "Heather was a pretty selfish bitch to tell you the truth. She made more money than me, but I still paid for all of our dates. She would sleep with me, then tell me how much she liked this other guy who lived in London, it was always about her and what she wanted and never about me and what I wanted!"

"Is that why you were threatening her on social media?"

Logan's eyes opened wide, and his face flushed.

"Listen, is that what this is about? I never meant any of those things I said, I would never do any of those things I might have said, I was, I was just venting, you know?"

"Were you in the city today?"

"Yes, I said I was."

"Did you see Heather today?"

"No, no, I didn't."

"What time did Jen come to your apartment this evening?"

"About six, I already told you that."

"Yes, but that's not true. Is it? You weren't with Jen until after eleven, possibly even midnight… Why would you tell me otherwise?"

"No, I, I was, we, we were? …I was home okay, I was, and I thought you might want an…"

"A what, Logan? An alibi?"

"I was home, I swear, I don't know why I said six, maybe it was eleven, I just don't know?"

"Did you see Heather Mills today, Logan?"

"Today? No, I couldn't, I mean no, no I didn't. Sorry, I, oh man, I'm getting a little confused. No, I didn't see her, I mean no … we're broken up and I don't go anywhere near there anymore, not for weeks."

"Anywhere near where?"

"Her apartment, I haven't been there in weeks."

"Where were you between seven and eight?"

"Home."

"Logan?"

"Home!"

"I think you saw Heather earlier, didn't you?"

"No, sir!"

"You went by her place at about seven, didn't you?"

"No, I was still on my way…"

"On your way? From where-to-where, Logan?"

"No, I mean, I mean, I, I… No. I was, might have still been on my way home from the city."

"From Heathers? – Did you kill Heather Mills today, Logan, did you as you so eloquently put it – 'End that bitch,' today, Logan?"

"No, sir, I wasn't anywhere near there."

Tommy and everyone in the observation room immediately took note of that answer, as he didn't question Heather's death, just his whereabouts.

"So, you're telling me again, you were nowhere near Heather's apartment on the East Side? And you had nothing to do with her death?"

"I was on the East Side, but no, I didn't see Heather today, I didn't… and her death? You think I killed Heather? Heather is dead? What is going on here… should I be asking for a lawyer? Heather is dead? And you think I killed her?"

"Did you?"

The back and forth went on for another half an hour, as Logan attempted but could find no reasonable timeline or proof of his whereabouts between leaving his last go-see on East 57th Street and meeting with Jen Arcola at 11:30 that evening.

With no viable alibi, it was decided that Logan would be held as a suspect in the death of Heather Mills. Once notified, Logan immediately asked for a lawyer.

Jimmy and Clay drove Jen Arcola home to her parents' house in Queens.

Tommy notified the district attorney's office that they were arresting Logan Mathews for the murder of Heather Mills and would be coming to get a search warrant for both Heather Mills's apartment and Logan Mathews' apartment, as well as subpoenas for both of their phone records.

William Tell

Chapter Four

Tommy's eyes opened to the dim light of the sun making its way around the dirty shade of the precinct's dorm window, and Clay's heavy breathing from the bunk below.

It was 7:28 AM. Tommy, Clay, and Doreen had opted to catch a couple of hours of sleep in the precinct's dorm rooms rather than go home, only to turn around for another day's work on Heather Mill's case. Although an arrest had been made, they still had a mile of work ahead of them to make their case.

There were now less than 24 hours left before Logan's arraignment; A search warrant needed to be executed on Logan Mathew's apartment, subpoenas required to be delivered for phone records, and today's autopsy of Heather, which Tommy already knew he would not witness personally, simply because of the time constraints with executing the search warrant.

9:01 AM

Tommy, Doreen, and Clay sat in a booth for breakfast at Niel's Coffee Shop on Lexington Avenue. After barely sleeping the night prior, the three looked worse for wear but were satisfied they had nabbed their man within just hours of the homicide.

The trio discussed the case in length as they finished their meals. They then drove downtown to the courthouse to swear out their warrant. They fought traffic across the bridge to make their way back to Logan's apartment in Astoria. They roused the landlord from his basement apartment to open the place up for them.

The detectives searched Logan Mathews' small, well-kept one-bedroom apartment for over two hours. During the search, they recovered a loaded .22 Caliber Baretta pistol under the mattress, four one-ounce bags of marijuana, and a plastic bottle with an RX label for amoxicillin, which instead contained fifty-seven blue tablets with SKY imprinted on them in his nightstand, coincidentally the same tablets found in Heather Mill's purse at the crime scene.

"Tell me this won't make this case?" Doreen said, shaking the bottle, making the pills rattle inside of it, "I bet he wasn't just her ex, I bet he was her supplier?"

The three were pleased with these discoveries. They felt strongly that the pistol would prove to be illegal, and the tablets would be Molly/Ecstasy, an illegal controlled substance.

The findings would enable the district attorney to hold Logan pending further investigation, but they were also a matching color and brand name to the pills found with Heather's body, another link in the chain tying Logan to this case.

The search ended at about 1:20 PM, and Tommy called the morgue to check in with ME Kristen Smyth to see if he should still make it over for the autopsy. She said yes.

To make their time a little more useful, Doreen and Clay dropped Tommy off at the morgue before they served the subpoenas for Heather and Logan's phone records.

2:12 PM

Tommy walked down the disinfected hallway of the morgue and met ME Smythe in her autopsy chamber, and after saying their hellos, she began.

"Okay, so we knew, or I should say thought, the cause of death was obvious for this one, and it was. The arrow killed Miss Mills, or more precisely, the crossbow bolt that was shot into her throat, at what I believe to be a fairly close range."

"Bolt? So that's the proper terminology, as opposed to arrow?" Tommy asked.

"Yes, for whatever reason, a short crossbow arrow is called a bolt, correct… and that is what killed her. Unfortunately, her body is clean of any other evidence, as far as I can see, regarding hair, fibers, or blood from any other individual. I see nothing that indicates a struggle or that she was struck by any object, fists, or anything other than the bolt in her neck, which caused her death."

"That is unfortunate," Tommy said with a sigh. He had hoped to gain more evidence.

"It does not appear that Miss Mills had any sexual relations in the twenty-four hours before her death. She did, however, have trace amounts of alcohol, marijuana, MDMA-Molly, and cocaine in her system. Not enough to make her drunk or high at the time of her death, but enough to lead me to believe she was a regular user of these products. Other than that, she was a truly healthy young woman… I'm sorry I don't have more for you, Detective."

"No, don't be sorry. I'm happy to report we have made an arrest for this murder, and now we're just wrapping up the case with everything we can collect to prove this is indeed our man. As always, thanks for everything, Smyth."

Tommy left the morgue and caught a cab back to the precinct. When he walked in the door, Sergeant Ruffalo called from behind the desk, "Hey, Keane! Captain wants to see you!"

Tommy turned from heading to the staircase and walked to the captain's office door instead. He then waited a moment so the sergeant could make the call and let Captain Pileggi know Tommy was to be knocking.

Once he got Ruffalo's head nod, he knocked on the door.

"Enter." Was heard from inside.

"Hey, Captain, how you doing? Sergeant Ruffalo said you wanted to see me?" Tommy stood just inside the doorway, hoping he wouldn't be asked to sit.

"Yes, Keane. I wanted to commend you on the quick arrest you and your team made on that homicide last night. Good work. That one would have, well may still, turn into a press case, but at least we're ahead of it, and from what it sounds, case closed as far as we're concerned."

"Yes sir, we have a suspect in custody. Found some damning narcotics evidence that may link him to the crime, as well as a firearm that will make sure we keep him in the system past arraignment as we tie this case up for the DA's office."

"Very good, Keane, keep up the good work."

"Yes, sir, thank you."

Tommy closed the door, and as he walked past the desk, he gave Sergeant Ruffalo a bewildered look and shoulder shrug, as gratitude and compliments were something new and unheard of from Captain Pileggi.

Tommy entered the Squad Room and found himself alone. He sat and took a moment to try to clear his mind in the quiet of the empty office. Forty minutes of quiet had passed when he could hear Doreen and Clay approaching.

"We got it, Tommy." Doreen began, "They were super helpful today, and unusually accommodating." She said as she held up a fat manilla envelope full of phone records. The three of them immediately tore open the packages, divided the paperwork up, and began searching through page by page.

Within an hour, they had recovered numerous incriminating texts between Logan Mathews and Heather Mills. These included phone sex, arguments, pleas by Logan to reconcile their relationship, several requests from Heather for both molly and cocaine, physical as well as death threats from Logan, over almost every disagreement imaginable. Theirs was a volatile relationship, to say the least.

The team highlighted every pertinent and damning communication between the two and forwarded them all to ADA Lokietz at the district attorney's office, the same ADA who had landed the Jenny Black (Lindel) case a few months earlier. Tommy was happy to have pulled her; he thought she was a thorough and competent young attorney.

The three detectives ended their tour satisfied with the fruitful evidence gleaned from the search warrant, autopsy, and phone records. All of which should make for an open and shut case and an easy conviction for the Logan Mathews arrest as far as the district attorney's office was concerned.

*****

The following morning, Tommy's eyes opened in the complete darkness of his room at his mother's apartment on 88th Street. The evening before, after what had transpired with the Heather Mills investigation, he did himself a favor and picked up a pizza from Italian Village after his tour. He and his mother, Maria, shared the pie and watched an old movie, The Man Who Shot Liberty Valance, starring John Wayne and Jimmy Stewart, on television. Tommy then went to bed early with little JoJo at about 8:30 in the evening.

He checked his phone; it was 6:14 AM, and he had slept for almost ten hours. He took a deep breath, stretched, and smiled to himself; nothing satisfied him more than a solid night's sleep.

As was his routine, he rolled out of bed and onto the floor for his fifty morning push-ups. Little JoJo perched on the side of the bed, trying to watch through the blackness as he did them.

Tommy felt fantastic. He hopped to his feet, threw on some sweatpants, and then took JoJo for a walk. When he returned, he found his mother awake and pouring her first cup of coffee of the day.

"Morning, Tommy. Can I fix you some breakfast, Tommy?"

"No, thanks, Ma. I'm heading out soon. I need to get downtown to court today, so I'll grab a little something on the way. Thanks."

He showered, shaved, dressed, and then walked down to the 2-1. He enjoyed the cool morning air during the walk, knowing his day would be easy, spent in court signing out the complaint against Logan Mathews with ADA Jessica Lokietz, whom he already knew and liked working with.

ADA Lokietz could not have been happier with the prospects of her day either. She appreciated her past encounters with Tommy and believed him to be a professional detective. She read through the Heather Mills case thoroughly that morning before he arrived. Although there were no eyewitnesses, and a weapon had yet to be recovered, it was a solid case. Tommy and the squad had documented and articulated the facts and timeline of their investigation perfectly.

The two reviewed the findings together and complemented one another on their fine work, ADA Jessica Lokietz, also informed Tommy that the judge decided Logan would be held in custody until the Grand Jury heard the case, where they would determine if he were to be indicted and stand trial for the 1st degree Homicide of Heather Mills, as well as the drug and gun charges.

Chapter Five

Day 7

Lieutenant Bricks stepped out of his office and into the squad room. He looked around at his detectives before taking a deep breath and announcing, "We got another one. Female body on East 90th near the Asphalt Green… And she's got an arrow in the back of her head."

"What?" Doreen said in disbelief, picking her head up from the file she was reading.

"Oh, fuck no," Tommy said in disappointment. Immediately fearing either a copycat or that they had made an erroneous arrest with the Heather Mills case, which would now give them two open murder investigations.

"Okay, listen up, whoever's catching tonight, you're not, this is most likely linked to Tommy's case with that young girl – So Tom, you're lead on this, I'm going to head up there with you… Sergeant Browne!" Lieutenant Bricks raised his voice to make sure he was heard.

"Yes, Lu?" Sergeant Browne answered as he stepped out of his office.

"We're all heading up to a homicide on 90th, you'll be here alone, keep an ear out for any calls, did you hear when I said…"

"Yes, another arrow killing, I heard."

"Alright, everybody, let's saddle up and head out."

***

9:10 PM
The Asphalt Green Sports Complex
555 East 90th Street

Tommy, Clay, Doreen, and Jimmy arrived on the scene first, with Lieutenant Bricks and Mark shortly behind them. The block had already been taped off, with three patrol cars, five officers, and a sergeant on location setting up and protecting the crime scene.

Sergeant Harrison, a short, dark-skinned woman with large light brown eyes, approached the squad as they exited their vehicles.

Harrison was new to the 2-1, a recent transfer from Queens, so she immediately introduced herself.

"Hi, I'm Sergeant Harrison. I just arrived two weeks ago, nice to meet you," she said hello and nodded to each of the detectives and Lieutenant Bricks. She was nervous; this would be her first time taking control of a crime scene, and the Lieutenant was in attendance. "We have a dead young lady, who looks to be in her mid-twenties. Shot in the back of the head with an arrow… I know you, I know we just had one of these a few days ago, another one, right?" She continued as they walked toward where the body lay, face down on the sidewalk, "Same M.O., yes?"

No one responded to her at first, as everyone took in the scene. Six sets of eyes were bouncing around, scanning the corpse and the immediate area for any obvious clues.

"Yes, it would appear to be the same M.O.," Lieutenant Bricks finally answered, still not looking at Sergeant Harrison but looking at the body as Tommy got closer and squatted down towards her head.

"What do we know, Sergeant?" Tommy asked, his eyes still fixated on the corpse.

"Nothing," Harrison answered, "We just showed up and started taping things off. No one has touched her, or anything near her since we arrived. We have the woman who placed the 911 call."

"Good. Who was first on the scene?"

"I was, and my driver, Officer Donaldson. It was Sector Eddie's call, but we arrived just before they did; we were only a couple of blocks away."

"Any witnesses? Where do we have the caller?"

"Uh, yes. Yes, to the caller, she is in the back of my patrol car, but no, no witness."

"Have you put in a call to Crime Scene or the Medical Examiner yet, Sergeant?" Lieutenant Bricks asked, still not making eye contact, his eyes fixated on the dead woman.

"Uh, no, should I?"

"No, I'll take care of it now."

Doreen squatted next to Tommy, "Same bolt with the same red flights, no way it's not the same guy."

"I'm right there with you, Doreen." Tommy took a deep breath and stood up. "Sergeant, how many of your people do we have on scene?"

"Six, if you include me."

"Okay, please, I see you already have someone posted on either end of the block. If I could get two of your people to take down every license plate on the block, please, and while doing so, keep an eye out for evidence. Have them look under each vehicle as they head up the block, as well. We want to ensure nothing was tossed under a car we may be interested in."

Tommy started to step away, then turned back toward the Sergeant.

"And if you and your driver can hold tight right here. Keep an eye on the body and another on our callers until I get with them, that would be great."

"Yes, yes, Detective, you got it." She replied.

"Jimmy, if you'd be so kind as to get all the names and shield numbers of everyone that shows up for my unusual report, please?"

Tommy continued,

"Mark and Clay. Please hit up each of the doormen here on the block. See if they saw or heard anything. Doreen and Lieutenant Bricks, I am going to spend a minute with our caller here, but I'm going to guess, looking at our victim and how she is dressed, there is a good chance she was either coming or going from the Asphalt Green here. Based on the direction she's facing, I will say leaving. Hopefully, they'll have some information on her, and I pray, some surveillance footage."

Everyone nodded, agreed with their current task, turned, and went to work. Tommy walked to the patrol car and opened the back door. A woman in her forties and what appeared to be her teenage daughter climbed out of the back of the sergeant's patrol car.

Tommy introduced himself, "Hello ladies, I'm Detective Keane from the 21st Precinct, so sorry you had to be a part of this tonight."

"Hello, Detective. I'm Mary, Mary Stuttgart, and this is my daughter, Dana." Both were dressed in gym attire with sports bags over their shoulders. Mrs. Stuttgart, was well-composed and well-spoken, but Dana was visibly shaken and nervously nodded along with everything her mother said.

"Please, dear, tell me what you saw," Tommy asked as he scratched their names in his notebook.

"We, my daughter and I, were leaving the Green, we had just been swimming, and as we came out and started up the block, I saw this girl, this poor girl, who had been shot... Shot with an arrow!"

"Do you know anything about this woman or what happened here tonight?"

Mary Stuttgart shook her head, "We don't know her personally. I have seen her here, once or twice, maybe. She was swimming here tonight, as were we, but no, I'm sorry, we don't know her. I'm sure they will inside, they'll be able to tell you who she is inside."

"Did you see anyone else outside? Anyone, or anything, suspicious when you left, or maybe even when you arrived?"

Mary Stuttgart and her daughter both paused and simultaneously shook their heads.

"No, sir, I'm sorry I can't think of anything. It was late and dark, and the block was empty when we stepped outside. To be honest, had we crossed the street, as we usually do, we would have never seen this poor girl's body."

"Thank you, thank you both for being so patient and so honest. Here is my card, in the event that anything at all, no matter how small, comes to mind, please call me. And the same goes for if you hear anything about this attack … maybe from the facility here or around the neighborhood, don't be shy to call me. You may go now, thank you." Tommy shook both of their hands and gently placed a hand on Dana's shoulder in an attempt to comfort her as he did.

While Tommy finished with the Stuttgarts, the Crime Scene Unit arrived, and Tommy pointed them toward the body. Tommy introduced himself as Jimmy took everyone's information for the unusual report.

Tommy stood close by and watched as the crime scene team did their job, taking photographs and measurements and looking all around the scene for anything they may deem possible evidence.

As he watched, Lieutenant Bricks and Doreen approached,

"Good news is they have some video footage for us, and we have a list of everyone who has been in and out of the building all day. Taking a look at our girl here, and the little we know from inside, I am going to guess that she will be a Miss Kaylee Reese." Doreen said.

"Alright, well that's something," Tommy replied.

As they continued to converse, Medical Examiner William Gannett approached and introduced himself. Once they got the heads-up from Crime Scene, M.E. Gannett and Tommy began to examine the body.

Gannett remained silent as he poked and probed around the body. He rolled her slightly to one side, retrieved a small gym bag from underneath her, and handed it to Tommy. In the bag's side pocket was a long, thin wallet with the victim's ID. It was indeed Kaylee Reese, a pretty, blonde, twenty-five-year-old from Groton, Connecticut.

Gannett finished his initial examination of Kaylee Reese and handed Tommy his card.

"I'm going to assume we all think this will be connected to the similar case you had a few days ago with Kristin Smyth?"

"At the moment I'm going to say yes," He replied.

"Give me a call in the morning and I'll give you an idea of what time to come down to the morgue, but regardless, we know what killed her."

"Yes, sir, I'll see you tomorrow."

"Good night, Detectives," Gannett said, nodding to them before leaving the scene.

Tommy and Doreen then conducted a thorough search of the body, which revealed no new or useful evidence. The body was then placed in a bag, removed by the medical examiners' techs, and driven off to the morgue.

Chapter Six

1:22 AM
168 East 89th Street, Kaylee Reese's residence.

Tommy and Doreen stood on the stoop of the red brick tenement and rang the bell marked Tollman/Reese.

"Yes? Who is it?" A woman's voice answered.

"It's the police, ma'am, Detectives Keane and Doyle, from the 21st Precinct. May we come up, please?"

The door buzzed, and they entered the building. As they climbed up the stairs, Tommy could see a young, dark-haired woman of about twenty-five, wearing a long T-shirt, standing in the doorway. She had a fearful look on her face, one of dread, of knowing something was about to happen that was not good.

"ID, please," she stated, while the two detectives were halfway up the last flight of stairs.

Tommy pulled his Detective Shield from his belt and held it high for the woman to see.

"Hello, Miss, Detective Keane. 21st Precinct. Detective Doyle is behind me. Does Kaylee Reese live here?"

"Oh my god… Yes, yes, sir, she does." A tear ran down the young woman's face. "What has happened to her? Why isn't she home yet?"

Tommy and Doreen stopped at the landing in front of the apartment's entrance.

"Your name, Miss?" Tommy asked.

"I'm Nicole, I live here with Kaylee, and another girl, Tara. Where? Where is Kaylee? What's happened?"

"I'm sorry to tell you, Nicole, your roommate Kaylee was found murdered earlier this evening over by the asphalt green. We'd like to come inside and speak to you and your roommate, Tara, if we may. We have a few questions that may help us with our investigation."

Nicole stood silent for a moment, dumbfounded in disbelief about what she had just heard.

"Murdered?" She took a deep breath and then repeated herself, "Murdered? Why? How? Who would do such a thing?" She paused again in disbelief before regaining some sense of the situation and invited the detectives into their apartment. "Yes, yes, please come in." As Tommy and Doreen stepped inside through the door, Nicole shouted, "Tara! Tara, get up and come out to the living room. The police are here about Kaylee."

The apartment was a respectable-sized, newly renovated space. The walls were painted white, with hardwood floors and one bare brick wall along the back. The unmatched furniture, empty pizza boxes, and Starbucks cups created the atmosphere of an unkempt college dorm room.

While the detectives scanned the room, another young woman, in her mid-twenties with long dark hair, exited her room, still pulling on a long bathrobe over her topless body.

"What's going on? Police? What happened? What happened to Kaylee?" Tara asked with a bit of panic and concern.

Nicole rushed to her and hugged her tightly, "Someone killed her! Someone killed Kaylee!"

Tara wrapped her arms around Nicole and tucked her head down into her shoulder, and they both began to cry.

"They need us to answer questions," Nicole said softly to Tara, then walked toward the couch in the middle of the living room. She moved a laundry basket and some blankets off it and asked the detectives to sit. She waved to Tara at the other side of the room, "Come sit, these detectives have some questions for us."

For about forty-five minutes, Tommy and Doreen questioned both girls about Kaylee's personal life, relationships, work history, and roommate situation. They were given contact information for Kaylee's mother and father, and then they were permitted to do a cursory search of the apartment and Kaylee's room.

All in all, Tommy and Doreen spent about an hour and a half with Nicole and Tara. Both women were forthcoming and helpful in every way.

After the interviews and search of the apartment, the detectives knew quite a bit about their victim: her relationship with her roommates, her boyfriend Michael, who was currently on a business trip to Chicago, her parents and younger sister, who all still lived in Groton Connecticut, and her job as a media rep for a large makeup company in midtown.

Unfortunately, the only thing they could gather from all this information was that Kaylee was a very well-rounded, well-behaved young woman who worked hard, loved her friends, family, and her boyfriend; barely drank, never did drugs, and as far as her roommates were concerned didn't have an enemy in the world, much less someone in her life who would intentionally shoot her in the back of the head with a crossbow bolt.

"She was bright and beautiful," Tara said, dabbing her red eyes with a tissue.

"Kaylee was perfect in every way, and we loved everything about her," Nicole added.

3:04 AM

Tommy and Doreen returned to the squad room to find Mark, Clay, Jimmy, and Lieutenant Bricks still investigating everything they could related to the case. They all convened in a circle in the squad room, some sitting in chairs, others on desks, discussing what they had learned, or not learned, regarding the case.

Clay began, "Jimmy and I went over every video we could find from the block and adjoining avenues, and so far, have found nothing of any use. Very few people were on the block then, and nothing directly on the crime scene."

Mark chimed in, "I ran Miss Reese every way I could and have found nothing linking her to anything of interest either. She seems like a fine upstanding citizen, no debts, no priors, nothing."

Tommy gave a short and simple description of the interviews of the roommates, "Seems like a charming young woman. Her roommates loved her, said she barely drank and didn't fool around with any drugs, had a long-time steady boyfriend who's currently in Chicago on business. Doreen and I searched her room and apartment, and found nothing sorted or out of the ordinary, seems like a terrific kid."

Lieutenant Bricks followed up, "I contacted the local PD in Groton, and they have notified the family. They intend to make the trip down tomorrow for an ID and an interview."

"Thanks, Lu." Tommy replied.

"So, what do we have here?" Lieutenant Bricks continued. "Seven nights ago, a young woman was killed with a crossbow in the hallway of her building on 82nd, now tonight we have another homicide, again an attractive young woman in her mid-twenties shot with a crossbow, this time on the street. Did we arrest the wrong guy the first time around? Or is this a copycat killing?

The room hung in silence for a moment, each detective heavy in thought, then Lieutenant Bricks began again.

"It's late, and we have a ton of work to do on this. Rather than plowing through, I'd like you all to get home, get some sleep, and have a proper meal. Tommy and Doreen, I want you two in for a 10-6 tomorrow and be prepared for a twenty-plus hour day. The rest of you come in at regular time, but we'll all be focused on this case unless we get hit with something big. It will be all hands on deck to try and make some headway on this one, understood? Kaylee Reese, and a revisit to the Heather Mill's case, we need to know if they are connected or a copycat."

Chapter Seven

9:44 AM

Tommy entered the squad room. He had gotten about three and a half hours of sleep at his mother's place on 88th Street the night before. Although it wasn't much, the comfort of his bed, the long hot shower he took, and fresh clothes made him feel somewhat rejuvenated. He was ready to begin digging into the Kaylee Reese case and reopening, or at least looking deeper into, the Heather Mills murder again.

The Squad room was empty except for Sergeant Barnes, the A team supervisor, who sat in his office reviewing his team's cases.

Tommy pulled the Mills case folder from the file cabinet, sat, and began making notes on a legal yellow pad. He drew a line down the middle of the page, then on the left wrote Heather Mills, and on the right, Kaylee Reese, then under each began listing their similarities; Mills, 28, from Ohio, wannabe actress, Only-Fans model, beautiful, lived within the confines of the 2-1, murdered with a crossbow.

Reese, 25, Connecticut, media work for a makeup company, beautiful, lived in the 2-1, crossbow.

At first glance, these women were almost identical, young, beautiful, from out of state, living in the same area, both killed by apparently matching crossbow bolts.

Under this list, he then wrote – CONNECTIONS?

Tommy thought to himself, 'If it turns out Logan Mathews didn't kill Heather Mills, who did, and what is the connection between these two girls?'

He stared at the yellow pad, and although he was thoroughly convinced of Logan Mathews' guilt after his arrest and interview, he had immediately begun to doubt it as soon as he stood over Kaylee Reese's body on 92nd Street.

Sure, it could be a copycat crime, but the Mills murder was only seven days old, and although it made every paper and was featured on New York One News, it didn't get the press coverage it could have. Tommy felt it was unlikely this new murder would turn out to be a copycat.

He diverted his attention from the yellow pad and opened the Heather Mills case folder, pulling everything out of it and reading over every sentence he had written.

Although the case was only a week old and still very fresh in his mind, he wanted to ensure there was nothing in the folder that might shed light on a different aspect or angle to the killing of Heather Mills.

As he read, his cell phone began to buzz. He looked down at the screen and saw it was Gil Nunez, the reporter from the Herald who had written about the Sister Margaret case and helped him with the Hayden Jon Marshall and Li Jun cases.

Tommy knew what Gil wanted - information on the Reese and Mills cases, no doubt. Tommy wasn't ready and didn't want to talk to Gil, but out of respect, he picked up the phone. "Keane here, " he answered.

"Hey Tommy, Gil here, how you doing? Can you talk?"

"Hey, how you doing? I'm in the middle of something right now pal, but go ahead, I got a minute for you, what do you need?"

"Doing alright, thanks. I am hoping you can share something with me about these crossbow killings. I understand you're lead on both of these, I know there was an arrest on the Heather Mills case, but what is the story now? Two dead girls, the same highly unusual weapon, in the same neighborhood a week apart, this has got to throw everything you thought about the Mill's case on its head?"

"To be honest my friend, right now I don't know what to think, and with the little I know and the new investigation just getting started, I have to refuse comment at this time, even for you, Gil."

"I understand. Kind of expected that. When I heard you were involved, I wanted to reach out before I wrote anything… I don't know if you saw any of the papers this morning, but the News is calling the perp the 'Crossbow Killer' and the Post has dubbed him 'William Tell'."

"No, I haven't. I'm going on three hours sleep after last night and have had nothing on my mind except this case since around 9:00 PM last night. But I tell you what, when I talk to anyone, it will be you."

"Well, thank you, sir, I can't ask for more than that."

"No, I owe you. When I have something worthwhile and real, you'll hear from me. Now let me get back to work. I have a lot ahead of me."

"Go do your thing, Tommy, and you don't owe me a thing," Gil said before hanging up, knowing that he owed the current status as his paper's number one crime reporter to Tommy, and the three cases Tommy had mentioned.

Just as Tommy started back into the Heather Mills case folder, Doreen stepped into the squad room. "Morning, Tommy, how you feeling today?"

"Morning, not bad dear, got next to nothing for sleep, and haven't eaten a thing yet. Just got up, showered, and rushed back here, you?"

"Same. I crashed for about four hours and was moving so slowly this morning, I took a cab rather than bother with the train," she continued as she sat at her desk with the cup of stale coffee she had just poured herself. "So, what are we thinking with these cases? Did we get the wrong guy for the Mills case?"

"I hate to say I'm thinking we might have, although everything we had pointed to Logan Mathews; the volatile relationship, the drugs, the phone calls, and text messages, the constant lying about his whereabouts... everything, absolutely everything pointed towards him, and it still could be him. At the moment, he is still our most likely suspect, but I gotta say, Doreen, after seeing that bolt sticking out of Kaylee Reese last night... Well, I don't know what to think now. The bolts appear identical, the circumstances identical, I started writing up a list comparing the two, and they are almost identical."

"That it?" Doreen motioned to Tommy's yellow pad, "Let me see what you got."

Tommy handed Doreen his pad, and she glanced at it as there wasn't much on it yet.

"They were also both blonde," she mentioned as she returned the pad to Tommy. He placed it down and quickly noted 'Blonde' in each column.

"Yeah, so I don't know what to think right now. My question, well, I have a lot of questions, but the big one I think for us will be connection. Can we find a connection between our victims? Did they know one another or have a friend or acquaintance in common? That may be what leads us to our killer. Why these two women? Forget about the odd weapon choice or proximity to one another. Why did our perpetrator target these two women? There must be a common thread between them."

"I agree, so where do we start?"

"Reinterview Kaylee's roommates, people at her job, and Heather's neighbor, do a deep dive into both of their lives online and question everyone we can as far as friends, family, people they know, and places they frequented. We'll just flip every stone we can until we find a connection, there has to be one, unless this is indeed a copycat crime, and at the moment I don't think it is."

"And what do we think about Logan Mathews?"

"We'll reinterview him, and I bet you anything, he'll be more forthcoming now that he is sitting in Rikers awaiting trial. And if we find he isn't somehow connected to Heather Mills' murder, he'll still be held pending the gun and drug charges making their way through the courts, in fact, that's even more leverage for the DA's office to use against him for his continued cooperation."

"Me think's we got a long day ahead of us, Mr. Man, where you want to start?"

"Bacon, egg, and cheese on a roll, right around the corner at Neil's?"

"I love you, Tommy Keane!"

Chapter Eight

The two walked down to Neil's Coffee Shop on Lexington Avenue. Tommy did indeed have a bacon, egg, and cheese on a roll with an iced tea, and Doreen had a BLT with a Diet Coke. They discussed their plans for the day.

Upon returning to the squad room, Tommy called and spoke to M.E. Gannett, and they decided to meet at the morgue at 1:30 to discuss the autopsy. They then put together a list of things that needed doing. Since the rest of the team would arrive a few hours later, they decided to hand over much of the initial computer searches, freeing them up so they could run around the city conducting interviews.

With phones and notebooks in hand, they headed out the door to learn as much as possible about Heather Mills and Kaylee Reese.

Their first stop was to revisit Irene Fisk, Heather Mills' neighbor at 407 East 82nd Street. They sat with her for about forty minutes. Irene had little to add since her initial interview. Although they were neighbors and friends, at sixty, Irene was thirty-two years older than Heather and only knew her from their occasional meetings in the hallway.

They had had coffee together a few times and did laundry at the same time, but they had never really opened up to each other. However, she was very forthcoming and gave them an interesting lead when she said that Heather took regular dance classes at the Steps Dance School on Broadway. She said she would go there three to five times a week for classes,

"It was a love of hers, and how she stayed so fit." She said.

After Irene's interview, they headed downtown to the morgue to see M.E. Gannett. He described the cause of death, which everyone already knew. He stated that Kaylee Reese was a healthy, athletic young woman and was negative for any drugs or alcohol in her system. He did add one interesting and crucial bit of evidence to the case when he stated,

"The two bolts used in the killing of Kaylee Reese and Heather Mills are of the same make; they are both 12.8-inch Ballista brand carbon bolts with red flights. Although they are the same brand and model, we have no way of knowing if they are from the same package, but I assume there will be a connection here."

At about 2:15 in the afternoon, Tommy and Doreen met with Tara O'Cain, one of Kaylee's roommates, whom they had met and interviewed just twelve hours earlier. Tara, who was also twenty-five, worked at a marketing firm on Third Avenue off 43rd Street. She took a break and made time for the detectives; the three sat in a meeting room used by the firm.

Tara was still somewhat in shock,

"I can't believe any of this. I don't even know how I made it here this morning, to be honest. I've been in a daze all day. I'm so happy my boss understands; she's asked me to go home, but I somehow don't feel right doing that either. I, we, Nicole and I cried for hours this morning, pretty much cried ourselves out, and then I just showered, dressed, and came to work. I mean, is this normal? What do people do when something like this, something bad like this enters their lives?"

"Everyone processes their grief differently, Tara," Doreen said.

"There is no right or wrong way," Tommy added, "Sometimes, doing exactly what you're doing works well for people. I know I'm that way. Get right back to life and right back to work. Keeping yourself busy can be an excellent coping mechanism."

Tara blew out a deep breath, "I don't know how well I'm coping just yet; I feel like I'm in a fog, I almost… I kinda don't even want to go back to the apartment to see Nicole. I just dread the idea of having to cry again."

Tommy and Doreen did their best to comfort Tara. Then, they asked her as many questions as they could about her personal life: relationships, hobbies, anything and everything they could to try and get to know her and what she did day by day and see if any interesting leads presented themselves.

The detectives took notes, but overall, nothing stood out.

Kaylee had a steady, long-term boyfriend who was currently out of town. She had no family in the city, and she lived with her closest friends, one of whom, Nicole, she had known all through college. She worked at the corporate office of a small boutique-style makeup company, managing their social media and organizing events.

Tara described Kaylee as a "fairly boring homebody, if she wasn't at her boyfriend's apartment, she was on our sofa with him sitting next to her watching an episode of Friends for the umpteenth time, and hobbies? The only thing she did was swim; she swam regularly, she competed in college and swam like four times a week at the Asphalt Green."

***

Their next stop was 168 East 89th, where they went to speak with Nicole Tollman once again.

Tara, whom they had just left, was taking Kaylee's death rather hard. As she said, she could not concentrate on her work and was "in a daze" all day, but Nicole was shattered.

When Nicole opened the door for Tommy and Doreen, it was evident to them that she hadn't slept. She wore the same long T-shirt from the night before and looked like hell had visited her. Although it was just over twelve hours after their initial visit, the lack of sleep, constant crying, and no eating or drinking in that short period had taken a toll.

Her face was pale and swollen, her eyes bloodshot, and her hair a complete mess. That simple long T-shirt looked as though it had come from the bottom of the hamper.

"Come in, please," she said, with a forlorn tone.

Nicole was asked the same series of questions Tara had been asked, and much of the information and general profile of Kaylee they had received from Tara's interview were the same. The only difference was Nicole's emotional state. She found it impossible not to cry while answering the different questions and continually asking the detectives over and over, "Why would someone do this to her?" and "Who could do this to her?"

Questions, of course, which were unanswerable, as these were the same answers Tommy, Doreen, and the rest of the squad were looking to ascertain.

They spent about forty minutes with Nicole, trying to comfort her as best they could. They then thanked her for her time and headed back downtown, this time to Kaylee's job at the Violetta Makeup and Healthcare Corp. on West 57th Street.

Upon making their way up to the corporation's 12th-floor office, they were greeted by the receptionist, a tiny, beautiful Italian girl with a heavy accent, dressed as if she were heading out for a night on the town and with make-up like a movie star. They asked if they could speak with a manager or supervisor.

"This about our Kaylee, yes?" she asked.

"Yes," Tommy answered, and the young woman picked up the phone and whispered into it, letting someone know to come to the desk.

Another woman, just as beautiful and about forty-five years old, opened the glass door leading to a hallway. She was dressed as if she would be hitting the red carpet in what appeared to be an evening gown and four-inch heels.

"Hello Detectives, my name is Margo. Please walk this way. May I offer you some coffee, tea, wine, or a soft drink?" she asked as she opened another broad glass door to a meeting room with a large table and about a dozen clear Lucite chairs.

"No. Thank you." Tommy replied.

"No thanks, not for me." Said Doreen, who was almost mesmerized by Margo.

Margo Violetta was an elegant woman. She stood about five feet nine inches tall, but her heels put her at about six feet one inch. She was in terrific shape and had long jet-black hair with a shock of bright white about three inches wide on the left side of her forehead. She wore her silky hair up on the sides and down in the back.

Margo was fifty-six years old, and although the maturity in her face made one think she was in her mid-forties, her figure was that of a twenty-five-year-old.

Tommy and Doreen were not only taken by just how stunning this woman was but also found it almost off-putting as her beauty seemed to get in the way of the conversation.

The three of them sat in the meeting room, and Tommy began asking a few simple questions about Kaylee and her job.

"Kaylee has worked for us for almost three years now, she is, I'm sorry, was, an absolutely fabulous employee. She was always on time, full of energy, a real go-getter, in fact…" Margo had to take a deep breath to keep her composure as she began to choke up. "This morning, we wondered why she was late, because Kaylee was never late. It was one of our IT team members who read about her death this morning and notified us. It has been quite the shock to our little family here, never would I have imagined anything like this happening to our Kaylee, she was beyond a beautiful person."

"You say that, Ms. Violetta, but I do have to ask if there is anyone, anyone at all here at work that she may have had any problems or disputes of any sort with?"

"No, absolutely not, she was well-liked by everyone."

"By chance, would you happen to know, or recognize this woman?" Tommy showed Margo a 5x7 headshot of Heather Mills.

"Oh, my, she is beautiful, isn't she? At the moment, no, I don't recognize her at all. I assume this is the girl from the first murder?"

"Yes, this is Heather Mills. She was killed eight days ago in the same manner as Kaylee… let me ask you, it's obvious you work with many beautiful women, models, actresses, and the like. Would you have a list of women you have worked with over the last few years? Also, if it's not too much, a list of people Kaylee may have worked with outside of this office, other vendors, media people, venues, and venue owners, I know she was in charge of several events you've put on."

"Do you think this may somehow be work-related?" Margo asked

"Really, Ms. Violetta…"

"Margo, please."

"Margo, I don't think anything yet, we're searching. We're desperately searching for something, anything, that may point us in the direction of someone responsible for this. And anything, no matter how small or inconsequential it may seem, could be the lead that points us in the right direction… Right now, we have nothing but two dead girls, and the only thing they share at the moment is that they were both remarkably beautiful young women who lived about ten blocks from one another."

"I see." Margo reached for the phone in the middle of the table, "Giulianna, come in here, please." She hung up the phone with her index finger, "Serena, come to the meeting room one, please." And then she put the receiver down.

The first to arrive was Giulianna, another stunning woman in a tight black dress and black pumps, her jet-black hair cut into a bouncy bob. Right behind her was the equally, if not even more beautiful Serena, who was not as tall as Giulianna but was built like Jessica Rabbit and had long red hair to match the comparison.

"Yes, Margo?" they both asked almost in unison.

"You two will be tasked today with going through Kaylee's files, both paper and computer, and listing everyone she has been in contact with through this office… I do not care how small or insignificant this person may seem. If there is a name and any contact information at all connected with, or to Kaylee, I want it on that list. I think I am clear with what I want, yes?"

"Crystal," they both replied, almost in unison.

"You will have a list sometime today, even if it's later this evening, Detectives."

Tommy and Doreen stared at Margo silently for a moment, almost overwhelmed by this truly impressive woman.

"Margo, we can't thank you enough. Here is my card. It has my cell and my email, where Giulianna and Serena can send whatever they find. Again, thank you for your support in this investigation."

"Yes, Margo, thank you so much for your assistance," Doreen added.

"I wish you luck, Detectives, please find the animal that did this to Kaylee and that other girl, and bring him to justice, that's all I can ask, we will support you in any way we can."

Tommy and Doreen stood silent once they got on the elevator, absorbing the almost surreal experience they had just had.

"Have you ever…?" Doreen began.

"What? Seen more ridiculously beautiful women in one room at the same time? No, I haven't!"

"Exactly, holy shit, any one of them would have been the most perfect woman I have ever seen, and then the next one would walk in the room."

"I tell you what, though, I got to give it to that Margo; she's got to be the sexiest woman I have ever seen. Her looks, her attitude, how she filled that room with authority, and I bet she's at least my age?"

"I bet she's got a few years on you, Tom."

"Yeah, you think so?"

"I do, definitely. And the sexiest woman you have ever met, huh? So, you like a bossy woman with a little authority, do you, Mr. Man? You never struck me as the submissive type?" Doreen grinned.

"Nah, Submissive I am not, but damn if that Margo asked me to get on my knees, I think I'd drop like a ton of bricks."

"Hmmm, me thinks my Tommy has a crush on teacher?"

"Me thinks you might be right!"

***

After leaving Violetta Makeup, Tommy and Doreen headed up to 2121 Broadway, where the Steps Dance School was located.

They arrived at Steps at about 6:45 PM. As they attempted to climb the stairs, a class seemed to be finishing up, and a dozen or more dancers made their way down.

Once upstairs, they ID'd themselves to a young woman at the reception desk. She had no answers to their questions but said it was okay for them to speak to any of the instructors in any one of the studios on the floor.

Tommy and Doreen entered one of the studios, where it appeared that those dancers had just left. They saw one of the instructors still finishing up, and they introduced themselves.

"Hello, miss…" Tommy began.

"Hello, may I help you? I'm sorry, but you're not to wear street shoes in here, please?"

"Oh, I'm sorry," Tommy said as he backed up slightly towards the door, "Yes, well I'm hoping you can help us," Tommy said as he showed the woman his detective shield, which he had clipped to his belt, "I'm Detective Keane, and my partner here is Detective Doyle, we're from the 21st precinct and we're looking for information on this woman." Showing her a photo of Heather Mills.

The instructor, a tall, lean, regal-looking woman of about fifty, stepped closer. "I know her, well, I don't know her, but I have seen her here for sure, yes, and she's taken my classes maybe a few times… I'm a little afraid to ask, Detective, why are you looking for her?"

"No, we're not looking for her, we know exactly where she is," Doreen answered.

"So? How can I help you?"

"This is Heather Mills; do you recognize her name?"

"Heather does sound familiar, but that's a fairly common name. I know she has taken some of my classes, but what do you need from me, Detective?"

"Heather was murdered last week, and we're just trying to learn more about her, and one of our previous interviews led us here; supposedly, she came here to take classes several times a week."

"Murdered? Oh my god, I'm so sorry to hear that. Oh my, that's awful news… I, I'm sorry I don't know more about her; I just know her face; she was a beautiful girl and seemed friendly; other than that, I know nothing about her."

"May I ask your name, please?"

"Lynda, my name is Lynda Griffin; I teach Jazz and Tap here, and… Wow, I can't believe we're talking about a murdered student; okay, wow, what do you think I can do to help?

"Do you know of anyone who was friends with Heather?

"No, not right away, I don't, let me ask Bobby, he's here now and just had a Modern class next door, here follow me."

As they stepped out of the studio, a long, lean man, barefoot in black cotton jogging pants and a blue sleeveless T-shirt with Dance or Die printed across the chest, exited the studio next to where they had just stood.

"Bobby!" Lynda said rather loudly and nervously.

"Hey, Lynda, what's up?"

"These two are detectives, they're looking for information about one of our students who was…" Lynda had to take a breath, "Murdered last week."

"Say what?"

"Yes sir, how are you? I'm Detective Keane, and this is my partner, Detective Doyle. Do you know this young woman here?" Tommy showed Bobby Heather's photo.

"Yeah… Yeah, I know her, it's ahh, Heather something? Heather…?"

"Mills," Doreen said flatly.

"Yeah, right, Mills, so someone killed her, you say?"

"Yes, sir. We're trying to piece together her life and see what we can learn about her, and a previous interview brought us here. Can you tell us anything?"

"Yes, well, not much, but she did come here kind of semi-regularly. She seemed like a nice, attractive girl, always well put together, but not much of a dancer to be honest. We did a little modern showcase with her several months ago. She did fine, but certainly not professional material."

"What can you tell me about this showcase?"

"It was a forty, forty-five-minute showcase, basically a modern dance recital, we had some musicians in to do live music, and each of the students did a trio routine, and one or two small group routines."

"So, she would have been pretty familiar with everyone in this showcase then? Would you say so?"

"Sure, some people get close, many you just know for the few weeks of rehearsals. I personally didn't know Heather really at all outside of her taking my classes maybe a dozen or more times, nice enough girl, but did seem to keep to herself from what I could see when she was here."

"Yes, I would say the same," Lynda interjected, "She was always charming and very polite. To me, she seemed more like a rec dancer."

"A rec dancer?" Doreen asked.

"Yes, a recreational dancer, interested in coming in more to work out, maybe learn to move more than to actually ever be on Broadway, it's not derogatory, it's just, well, they aren't here as professionals."

"Okay, got it." Doreen replied, "Is it possible to get a list of her classmates in this showcase? Hopefully, one of them will know a little more about Heather and be able to help us with our investigation. We have so many unanswered questions, and so far, no one to ask."

"Yes, we should have an old program from that date. Let me check for you … just give me a minute." Bobby turned and left the area. The entranceway they stood in began to fill with dancers coming in off the street and preparing for the next class. Doreen and Tommy backed up toward the wall and waited.

"Here you go," Bobby shouted, to be heard over the dozen or so dancers chatting as they stretched and prepared for class. "I knew we had a few of these flyers left. Here's a complete list of everyone who took part. I jotted down all the phone numbers I could find that we had next to the names, so here you go: twelve names and nine numbers. If you give me a call tomorrow, I will, or should, have the other three numbers for you."

"Bobby, Lynda… Thank you so much. You have been a tremendous help today; we really do appreciate it." Said Tommy as he shook hands with both instructors.

Doreen nodded, "Yes, thank you both."

After leaving Steps, Tommy and Doreen drove up to the Hi-Life restaurant on the corner of 83rd Street and Amsterdam Avenue. They parked at a bus stop and entered the stylish little bar and grill. They were greeted by a young woman in her mid-twenties who asked if they would like to sit indoors or out. Doreen immediately asked to be outside, but Tommy said no and shook his head.

"I can't sit outside. I don't want to eat with car and bus exhaust going by or some homeless guy interrupting our meal asking me for a buck or two." Tommy turned toward the hostess. "We'll take a table inside, please."

"Okay, Mr. Man, inside it is." Doreen quipped.

"Right this way then." Said the waitress. She walked them to a two-top, and Tommy sat on the banquette with his back against the wall under a picture of three old-time Burlesque dancers.

Doreen ordered tuna sashimi with an avocado salad and a Diet Coke, and Tommy ordered the half chicken with mashed potatoes and carrots.

The two sat and discussed their day. They were happy with the information and leads they had received from their interviews; however, both were disappointed they hadn't been put on the trail of a serious suspect yet.

The conversation turned to the Logan Mathews arrest. On paper, he was still the guy they liked for the Heather Mills case, but with this new victim arising, they were confident he was no longer the prime suspect in her homicide. They believed that the same perpetrator almost certainly committed the two homicides and could find no connection between Logan and the second victim.

Tommy called Lieutenant Bricks to inform him where he and Doreen were with their interviews and that they would return to the house soon to brief him.

Chapter Nine

9:12 PM
2-1 Precinct Squad Room

Tommy and Doreen stepped into the squad room, a little more than eleven hours after starting their shift. Although they were no closer to knowing who the killer of Heather Mills and Kaylee Reese was, they were satisfied with the number of interviews they had conducted and the number of names and leads they had garnered.

"Hey, how'd you guys make out today?" Clay asked as he noticed the two enter the room.

"Eh, no new developments, but we do have a list of names to get with for both victims. Hopefully, one or two of them will cast some light on these homicides, but as of right now, we're no closer."

"Same here. I been banging away on the computer here looking for anything on either of these two girls, but I haven't come up with much. Mark and Jimmy have taken the Reese girls' Mom and Dad down to the morgue for a positive ID.

They should be returning any minute now, so you can talk to them too."

"Tommy!" Lieutenant Bricks shouted from inside his office, "You and Doreen, come let me know what you got today!"

Tommy made eye contact with Doreen and nodded toward the Lieutenant's office as they walked toward his door.

"Come on in, sit, and tell me where we're at with these cases." Lieutenant Bricks said as he moved a case folder from in front of him and placed it to the side.

"Overall, Lu, we made some headway. I'm sorry to say nothing solid, and no connections between these two victims as of yet, but we do have several, well, more likely dozens of new names to look into who were in contact and knew these girls." Tommy replied.

"Yeah, Lu, it should be quite a bit. We just walked in, so we haven't checked our emails yet, but we expect lots of names to be delivered tonight, on top of what we've already collected today." Doreen added.

"Okay, all sounds good. I know you two are on it. Let me give you a heads up, Captain Pileggi is a little bent out of joint that we got the wrong guy in the Mills case, and that the second murder occurred. I explained that all roads led to Mathews and that, although I don't believe so, he may still be our guy. But regardless, he's being held on the gun and drugs charges, so we have time to work this case in every different direction it may lead. Nonetheless, you'll hear from the captain, and he's not happy. Also, he was asking about referring this to the homicide task force. We'll wait on that until we see what we can come up with here in-house."

"I appreciate your confidence in us, Lu, but know I have no problem with any assistance the Homicide Task Force can provide. There's no ego to be stepped on here; I just want to catch this creep."

"I know, Tom, but it's only been a day. Let's see what you guys come up with. Hopefully, you'll nail this filthy savage soon."

Clay knocked on the door sill to interrupt the conversation, "Sorry, Mark and Jimmy just returned with the Reese parents, if you're ready for them."

Tommy and Doreen stood up, stepped into the squad room, and approached Kaylee Resse's parents. Both were nicely dressed: Mrs. Reese in a navy pantsuit with a white blouse and Mr. Reese in a navy blazer, cream polo, and khaki pants. They looked like they would have been out for a lovely evening, maybe for dinner and a show, rather than going to the morgue to identify their slain daughter.

Although dressed nicely and with perfectly done hair, both wore grey complexions as if they were lifeless corpses themselves, walking across the room to greet Tommy and Doreen.

The four introduced themselves, entered the interview room, and sat down to discuss the Reese's beloved, now deceased daughter, Kaylee.

They talked about Kaylee for almost an hour, and her parents came to tears several times. Tommy and Doreen could tell this was a respectable, devoted, loving family, and had no doubts that she was everything she appeared to be on the outside: a hardworking young woman who didn't have anything to do with drugs or any other nefarious activities and apparently had a solid relationship with a nice man who loved her very much.

Unfortunately, the interview with Mr. and Mrs. Reese did nothing to enhance the investigation into their daughter's death; in fact, it seemed to raise two significant questions. Why would anyone want to kill Kaylee Reese? And what would the correlation be between Kaylee and Heather?

On paper, two women were living noticeably different lives: Kaylee, a homebody with a serious boyfriend, a secure career, a loving family, and loving roommates. And Heather, an Only-Fans model, was in a tumultuous relationship with a drug-dealing, gun-toting young man, who regularly threatened her, but who was also incarcerated during the Reese murder.

'Where is the connection?' Tommy thought as they finished their interview with Mr. and Mrs. Reese. And once they said goodbye, He asked it out loud to Doreen and the room in general.

"Where's the connection? That's our key! There must be… There has to be a link between these two girls - if we find that, we find our killer!"

Travis Myers & Natasha Myers Marsiguerra

William Tell

Chapter Ten

The Squad had worked late into the night, and Tommy was entering his fifth hour of sleep at his mother's apartment on 88th Street when his phone began to buzz on the nightstand.

He picked it up and saw that the time was 7:56 AM and that it was Gil Nunez again, so he answered it.

"Morning, Gil. How you doing?"

"Doing good, I hope I'm not waking you?

"You are, but that's okay. I assume you're calling for a reason?"

"Yes sir, I am. You're going to want to hear this."

"What? What you got?" Tommy perked up a bit as Gil's comment did indeed raise his interest, and he attempted to rub the sleep from his face.

"We got a letter this morning, and from what I understand, all four major papers received letters today from the man who claims to be responsible for the Mills and Reese killings."

"Get the fuck outta here? Really?" Tommy sat straight up in bed and asked in disbelief.

"Really. I haven't made it into the office to see it yet, but the editor called me right away. After the last few articles I wrote on your cases, the editor immediately called me to cover this one… So, what do you want to do? You want to meet me at the paper?"

"Yeah, yes. Yes, I do. Give me a bit to get myself together and make a few calls, and I'll come see you at your office."

"Cool, take your time. I need to do the same. Figure an hour at least before I arrive. See you there!"

"I'll see you there."

Tommy turned on the light and saw little JoJo sitting at attention, staring at him. He gave him a pet, then stretched his shoulders one way and then the next. He was beat. He hadn't slept a whole night in days, and here he was up and out again without a full five, never mind a full eight. He stood up, decided to forgo his usual fifty push-ups, and shuffled himself to the bathroom, little JoJo the shadow behind him.

"Good morning, Tommy." He heard his mother say from her recliner as she exhaled the smoke from a recent drag on a cigarette.

"Morning, Ma," he mumbled in reply as he entered the bathroom, started the shower, and then brushed his teeth.

Tommy dressed, walked JoJo, kissed his mother on the head, wished her a good day, and walked up to 2nd Avenue to catch a cab, but he still wasn't awake. He felt like one of the walking dead from some zombie movie, walking half-speed, still in a fog and lost amid all the week's happenings: the victims, interviews, stress. Over the last few days, his lack of sleep was beginning to hamper his performance.

He grabbed a can of Pepsi from a newsstand before hailing a taxi to the Herald on 35th and 6th to meet with Gil, hoping the sugar and caffeine would give him the boost he needed to get his morning started. As he sat in the cab, he texted Lieutenant Bricks to tell him he was starting early and had a lead at the Herald. Then, he called the precinct and had them sign him in.

He leaned against a car outside the building's entrance and texted Gil, 'I've arrived, and I'm outside.'

Gil responded, 'Wait there, I'll be there in less than five.'

Tommy got a second Pepsi from a corner coffee and doughnut vendor and waited.

***

9:22 AM

Tommy and Gil sat in a small meeting room on the fourth floor of the New York Herald. They were met by two of the paper's prominent editors and two other reporters. The editor-in-chief, Robert Blume, closed the door to the office and, before sitting down, began to speak,

"What I have here is a letter addressed to me, and from what I understand, it went to the editors of all the major city papers today… It's supposedly from a man who claims to have killed Heather Mills and the other girl, Kaylee Reese."

He paused as he handed out copies of the letters to everyone present. Blume moved to the head of the table and maneuvered his large, flabby body into the chair before continuing.

"Detective Keane, first let me thank you for coming so quickly. I have admired your work. You are an impressive credit to the police department, Detective, and I am delighted to have you here today."

"Thank you, sir," Tommy replied.

"As I'm sure you can imagine, we here at the Herald regularly get many strange letters, confessions, threats, and the like. Most of these are from kooks and trolls, and we pay little attention to them. However, this one may be real, and of course, if it is, it will be of interest to you, Detective. I think the last line will let you know if this letter is from a credible source."

The room hung silent as everyone sitting around the large table read their copies of the handwritten note, and the gravity of what they were reading set in.

TO WHOM IT MAY CONCERN

I AM A LITTLE DISAPOINTED IN THE LACK OF MEDIA ATTENTION I HAVE GARNERED WITH THE KILLINGS OF THE TWO BITCHES SO FAR !!

I DO HOWEVER LIKE THAT YOU HAVE ATTEMPTED TO NAME ME — BETWEEN "WILLIAM TELL" AND THE "CROSSBOW KILLER" I CHOOSE WILLIAM TELL, I DO LIKE A GOOD LITERARY REFERENCE

I WANT TO INFORM THE CITY THAT THIS IS NOT THE END, BUT ONLY THE BEGINNING OF MY REIGN, THERE WILL BE MORE DEAD BITCHES, AND MY LIST KEEPS GROWING !!

THERE IS NO SHORTAGE OF RUDE
BITCHES IN THIS CITY!!

TO THE NYPD - I HAVE NO DOUBT
YOU WILL CATCH ME, ALL THE
GREATS ARE EVENTUALLY
CAUGHT, I LOOK FORWARD TO
OUR CAT AND MOUSE GAME
UNTIL IT ENDS,

BE VIGILANT!!
I PLAN TO CONTINUE FOR SOME
TIME,

YOURS TRULY
WILLIAM TELL

P.S.
FOR THE NYPD, TO KNOW MY
AUTHENTICITY, BOTH BITCHES
WERE SHOT WITH 12.8"
BALLISTA BAT BOLTS WITH
RED FLIGHTS —
I HOPE THIS CONFIRMS MY
AUTHENTICITY TO YOU, TO
MY KNOWLEDGE NO ONE
HAS REPORTED THIS FACT
AS OF YET,

"Detective Keane," Robert Blume began, "No one has reported on the bolts used, is this… Is this William Tell correct? Do you believe he may be the killer?"

"Yes, he is correct, and it appears he very well may be the individual we are looking for."

Tommy took his phone out of his pocket and called Lieutenant Bricks, raising his right index finger to Blume to let him know to pause for a moment.

"Hey, Lu, Listen, I'm down at the Herald. They have a letter here that appears to be legit from our killer. It says he's not done yet, and he's got a list; he's even challenging us to catch him… Yeah, sure, what say you bring the captain with you if you can, they can ask him questions in person… Yes, sir, I'll secure the note now and wait for you and the captain. Very good, Lu; see you in a bit."

Tommy put his phone down and then began to address the room.

"Okay, yes, I believe this letter may be authentic. I will have to take the original, and please don't touch it again. We'll retrieve it from wherever it is and send it to the lab. It would appear we may have a psychopathic serial killer on our hands. My lieutenant and captain are on their way here. This way, we can conduct our initial press briefing right here in this office. Is that doable, Mr. Blume?"

"Yes, we can do that."

"Very good. These cases have taken a turn here this morning, and I have no idea where they will go now regarding an investigation, but we can all agree it will be a big deal. What I would like to propose to you is for your cooperation, Mr. Blume. As a paper, will you be willing to work with us and assign Gil here to the story? I promise I will work with him exclusively and honestly. I will share any information we deem printable with him, but at our pace, and expect any information you receive to be delivered to me promptly before its printed, so we can decern what is important to our investigation and hopefully you will be recognized as the paper who delivers the truth in this case rather than the bullshit hype that has already begun and is sure to continue. This agreement, of course, does not leave this room, even to my superiors, as there's no need for that, and it would only hamper our relationship, but the moment I feel the Herald has stepped outside of the truth is the moment my cooperation ends."

Robert Blume paused for a minute. He stood up, walked around the table, stuck his hand out, and shook Tommy's.

"Absolutely, it would be an honor to work with you, Detective Keane, and you have my word that anything our investigation reveals will go to you before it goes to press."

"Thank you, sir, this is going to be a big case and a big story, please, let's all work together to not fuck it up, and hopefully, bring it to a swift end."

***

10:44 AM

Captain Pileggi, Lieutenant Bricks, and Officer Ortiz arrived at the Herald and went to the meeting room where Tommy, Gil, and Robert Blume waited.

Tommy raised his head and asked Gil and Blume if they could have the room.

Then, he waved Captain Pileggi and Lieutenant Bricks into the room and motioned for them to sit down. Captain Pileggi looked frustrated and angry, which was nothing new and to be expected. What surprised Tommy was that he stayed silent and took his seat without saying a word.

"Captain, Lu, I got a call just a couple hours ago to come here to authenticate this letter," Tommy passed each of them a copy of the letter, as they both read it, he continued, "It looks like we have a serial killer on our hands, as you see he says he has a list, and he's not done… I do believe this to be a real letter. Why? Because the manufacturer, the length, and the color of the bolts used are correct, and as the writer says here, that was never printed in any of the papers, so how else would he know?"

Tommy and the room remained silent for a moment. Tommy continued, "I think the right, or the only, course of action will be to get the Homicide Task Force involved to give us the additional manpower this case will need. Lu, I assume I will remain with this case as it was mine initially. I'd like you to decide if I can keep any of our people on this with me, and if I can, I would request Doreen. We work well together, and she makes up for some of my technical shortcomings. This case has just become huge gentlemen, everyone is going to be up our asses to catch this guy, and to stop any more of his promised killings. I don't think I'm being out of line when I say we need to proceed quickly and properly, we have potential lives to save."

Tommy almost added 'careers to save,' to help shove Pileggi in the right direction, but thought that may be a bit too much and a little insulting, even though he knew it would be in the front of Pileggi's mind.

"I agree with Tommy, Captain, we'll have to get with Homicide and set up a separate task force for this case immediately. The press is going to go nuts with this one," Lieutenant Bricks said, not only because it was the truth but because he knew the word press would jolt Pileggi into action.

"You are both one hundred percent correct, we want to get out ahead of this thing as much as we can, and if we're going to save any souls, we need to bring this William Tell asshole to justice as quickly as possible. Lu, I'll lay this in your lap to coordinate, and Keane, I do think it's prudent that we keep our best man on this case. I know we got the wrong man with the first victim, but as Lieutenant Bricks said, all roads led to him, and I am inclined to believe that is the case, so let's get to work and catch Mr. Tell here." Pileggi stated.

"Very good, Captain. The Herald has a reporter waiting and would like to speak to both of you if he can. I assume you would like to give them a little something after they did us the courtesy of calling us in here before going to press with the letter." Tommy explained.

"Yes, yes, of course, bring him in."

William Tell

Tommy stepped outside and waved Gil into the room. There, he interviewed Captain Pileggi and Lieutenant Bricks, adding several quotes from each in his story about the William Tell letter that would go to press in the paper's next edition.

Chapter Eleven

The three men and Officer Ortiz returned to the 2-1, and Lieutenant Bricks and Tommy spent the rest of the day setting up what would become the William Tell Task Force.

Manhattan North complained of manpower and space shortages but could commit three detectives to the team: Detective 1st grade Joseph Hanrahan, Detective 2nd grade Therese Voss, and Detective 2nd grade Miguel Ortero. Lieutenant Bricks gave Tommy Doreen, as per his request, and he added Jimmy Colletti since Jimmy was being taken out of rotation anyway, pending being called to the Sergeant's course. They were also given two designated administrative assistants, PAA Gloria Di Nunzio and PAA Brenda Lotts.

This gave the case six investigators and two PAAs. Regarding office space, Captain Pileggi had a storeroom on the fourth floor emptied. It was small and only had one window facing a brick wall in the alley, but it could fit six desks and two filing cabinets. It was out of the way and removed from the precinct activities, and it kept everything private, secure, and within the walls of the 2-1.

Lieutenant Bricks remained on as the administrative supervisor. All of this went smoothly, but it took two days to set up. During this time, only Tommy and Doreen could work the cases. They concentrated on interviewing everyone they could from the lists provided by Kaylee's office and Heather's dance school, but nothing of investigative value was gleaned over those days.

***

It was 9:50 in the morning. Tommy had brought in bagels and coffee from H&H Bagels. The task force was scheduled to meet for the first time as a team this morning. It was decided they would work 10:00 AM to 8:00 PM shifts daily and, of course, stay as late as needed each evening. Two detectives took days off at a time, so there would always be at least four detectives on the case at all times.

Their office was tight, so this initial meeting was held in the muster room. Tommy was in first and began setting up the bagels and coffee. Soon, Doreen arrived with Lieutenant Bricks, then Miguel Ortero, a short, round man with a receding hairline. Miguel was the consummate ballbreaker with a broad smile and an infectious laugh. It was impossible for him not to crack a joke whenever one presented itself.

The next in was Therese Voss. She stood about 5' 7", was thin, and wore a sharp navy pinstripe suit. Her face was becoming, especially for her age, but she carried the dead eyes of a woman who had worked hundreds of homicides.

Jimmy Colletti and Joseph Hanrahan arrived simultaneously. Joseph was a huge man who stood 6' 4" and weighed 302 pounds. His hair was more salt than pepper, and his white mustache covered his entire mouth. He wore a navy sport coat over navy Dickies work pants and black sneakers. He was a mess to look at, but at that time, he had cleared more homicide cases than any other detective in the city.

Gloria Di Nunzio and Brenda Lotts were the last to arrive. Gloria was a thirty-two-year-old pistol from Bensonhurst who was somehow lost in the late 1980s. She was a small and thin statured woman but everything about Gloria was big; she had big hair, big gawdy jewelry, big brown eyes, a big attitude, and a big mouth that could be heard across any room even when she would exaggeratedly put one of her hands, with her very long very bright fingernails over it to whisper a not so quiet whisper. Gloria was a character who regularly assisted the Homicide Task Force, and all the members loved her.

Brenda Lotts, was a more modest looking dark skinned woman of forty-seven, who lived her entire life in the same apartment she was born in on East 122nd Street and as it would happen went to the same high school as Tommy, although neither remembered one another from there, however, Brenda did recall the incident where Terry Calahan had stabbed one of the Cigar Mob Gang to death in the boy's bathroom.

Lieutenant Bricks knew Joe Hanrahan and liked him. He introduced himself to Therese Voss, Miguel Ortero, Gloria Di Nunzio, and Brenda Lotts, then introduced everybody around and asked them to take a seat. He quickly briefed them all about where they were on what was now called the William Tell Case. As they all enjoyed a bagel and some coffee, Jimmy passed out a case dossier for everyone to familiarize themselves with.

A rotating tour schedule was written up and implemented, and then all involved moved to the fourth floor, where the official William Tell task force was located.

"Holy shit, its tight in here!" The big man, Joe Hanrahan, exclaimed, "But we'll make it work."

"You four, go ahead and choose your desks. Jimmy, Doreen, and I can share one. We're used to having no place to sit, and besides, you're our guests for as long as this case lasts," Tommy said.

"I knew I was gonna like you!" Miguel said as he stepped into the long, narrow room.

Most of the day was spent updating the new team on what had transpired with both homicides and looking ahead at what was left to do.

The team also received visits from FBI Agent Janice Colandro, a profiler that One Police Plaza sent up who tried to create a profile of who they may be looking for, and handwriting expert Dr. James Finney, who went over the details of the letter after examining it.

Come the end of the day, they had little more to go on. Agent Colandro concluded that the perpetrator would most likely be a sexually psychopathic narcissistic male, white, between twenty-five and thirty-five years of age.

Dr. Finney said the way the letter was written was not conducive to examination because the letters were intentionally and aggressively scratched into the paper; however, did say there was a good chance that the perpetrator may be left-handed.

So again, at day's end, Tommy had nothing but several new and highly experienced eyes to look deeply into this case, and he was grateful for that.

William Tell

Chapter Twelve

Day 11 8:18 PM

It was the first day of Tommy's RDOs (Regular Days Off); as it happened, it was his first day off of the last six. He had worked both of his previous two RDOs, trying to get some headway on this double spree of killings that had started almost two weeks prior.

Tommy waited with Molly for an order at Charlie Mom Restaurant on York Avenue when his phone went off.

"Keane," he answered. "Oh no, fuck me, I don't believe it… Yes, yes, of course, I'll be right there."

Molly looked up at him. "That doesn't sound good?" she asked softly.

"No, another girl has been murdered."

"The, that, that arrow guy?" she asked nervously.

"Yes." He said flatly as he paid for their food.

Tommy walked Molly back to her place and up the stairs, gave her a solid kiss, and said, "I don't want you leaving the building. I know you gotta do things and you have to work, but stay off the streets at night, alright. Please keep your eyes open and your wits about you at all times. When you leave the bar, make sure someone walks you, or at the very least, you take a cab, I know it's only a couple of blocks, but I don't care. Stay off the streets if it's dark."

"I'll be safe, Tommy, I promise. You know I'm smart and…"

"Listen to me, Molly, I know nothing about what's going on with this killer, and to tell you the truth, he's scaring me. We have nothing on him yet, and now here we are with another dead girl within two weeks of the first, just please, be smart and for god's sake stay safe."

"I will," she said, giving him a tight hug, then a hard kiss on the mouth, before stepping into her apartment and locking the door.

9:02 PM
217 East 73rd Street Apartment 3D

Tommy arrived at the address Lieutenant Bricks had directed him to. He passed the officers in front of the building and went up the stairs to 3D.

"Hey Tommy, how you doing? Looks like this is gonna be your baby here." Detective Keogh's prominent voice sounded as soon as Tommy entered the apartment.

There, in front of him in the doorway of her apartment, lay the body of another beautiful blonde woman, who couldn't have been more than twenty-six, twenty-eight years of age. She was dressed nicely in a royal blue skirt and blazer, over a black, tight-fitting turtleneck. Her high heels were still on both feet, and like Heather Mills, she lay flat on her back, staring up at the ceiling, one eye open, the other with a crossbow bolt with red flights sticking out of it.

Keogh began again, "Jenna Morrison, twenty-eight years old, works as a realtor and rents apartments. A neighbor, Mr. Fleener, from upstairs, found her. He was coming home with his daughter. A little girl, eight years old, ran ahead, and she was the first to see this.

As Tommy squatted over the body, he heard the voice of Therese Voss, "Voss, I'm with the William Tell Task Force." Tommy stood and turned to greet her,

"Hey, Therese, how you doing?" he introduced her to Keogh, "Keogh, this is…"

Detective Keogh interrupted, "Therese Voss, how the hell are you, kid?" he asked as he hugged her. "Me and Therese go back, and good for you! You pulled a good one here. Therese is top-notch, brother; be happy she landed on your team." He then continued, "I notified everybody already, Tommy. Both Crime Scene and the Medical Examiner are on the way. I don't know much more than I've told you, but we'll be here until you tell us otherwise if you need anything."

"Thanks, Keogh, I appreciate it."

Crime Scene arrived and did their thing, just like with the Heather Mills case. Tommy had them dust all three staircases and hallways leading to Jenna's apartment for prints, as well as the stoop and entranceway. Moments later, ME Kristen Smyth from the medical examiner's office arrived and stated the obvious,

"She's dead, crossbow bolt to the eye is what did it."

Joe Hanrahan showed up and slowly examined everything he could at the scene, as did Therese Voss. All three interviewed the neighbor, Mr. Fleener, and his daughter to no avail. Therese later commented that Mr. Fleener was much more upset than his eight-year-old daughter, who seemed to be taking on more of the adult role in the relationship and comforting him.

Doreen then arrived and, with Keogh and Volpe, canvassed the block, speaking with doormen, neighbors, shop owners, everyone and anyone they could, but no one had anything to say. They were able to recover videos from two locations and, therefore, had some hope of finding something.

Jimmy showed up and was tasked with going through every trash can on the block and taking down every license plate, which he did with the assistance of Officers McEnroe and Williams from patrol.

After the Crime Scene was finished, Tommy, Doreen, Therese, and Joe conducted a cursory search of Jenna's small studio apartment to ensure everything was safe and secure. Although she had a cute place, the detectives found nothing of interest and would wait for a warrant to investigate her personal belongings.

All in all, they spent about five and a half hours at the scene, then the five Detectives returned to their office in the 2-1 to discuss and plan for the next day's investigation.

***

9:34 AM

Tommy arrived at the William Tell Task Force office with coffee and bagels to find Therese and Gloria already in, both reading through paperwork concerning the cases.

"Good morning, ladies."

"Good morning, Detective Keane," Gloria answered, dropping her chin and looking over her glasses at him with a cheerfully inviting, almost come-on smile and a wink. "How you doing today?"

Tommy, who was incredibly tired as he was entering his eighth straight day of work and had only three hours of sleep from the night before, had to smile back at her positive, somewhat sexual energy, something he wasn't prepared for. This was coupled with the fact that Gloria, even when dressed down in a simple velour tracksuit and sneakers, had a way of always not only looking her best but of carrying that air of 'looking to meet.'

So, he smiled back at Gloria, "As good as I can be, on three hours' sleep."

"Yeah, I'm hurting too." Said Therese, not glancing up from whatever it was she was reading.

"Oh, look at you… Aren't you a doll bringing in some coffee and bagels? Thanks, Detective. You are so sweet!" Gloria exclaimed.

"Coffee!" Therese now took notice and perked up. "Bless your soul, Keane. I knew I was going to like working with you."

Turning to Therese and lowering her voice as much as she could, Gloria said, "I knew I was going to like working with him the first time I laid eyes on him."

In light of the new murder in the case of Jenna Morrison, everyone on the team would be coming in for the day. Slowly, each of them arrived one by one, and they grabbed a bagel and a cup of coffee. Tommy's phone went off as they began to get organized and parse out everyone's duties for the day. Seeing that it was Gil Nunez, he immediately picked it up.

"Hey, Gil, what's up?"

"Morning, Tom, we received another letter from William Tell, I assume…"

"I'll be right there. Same building, same office?"

"Yes, sir."

"Be there as soon as I can!" Tommy hung up with Gil and told the team, "We got a new letter from our killer. Who's coming?"

All six of the detectives began to move when Lieutenant Bricks chimed in,

"Hold on, we don't all need to go see this letter. Tommy, Doreen, Joe and Therese head on down, the rest of you will concentrate on other aspects of last night's homicide, all the fun stuff like reviewing any video we may have, running all the license plate numbers, cross referencing any of the witnesses statements with statements given from the last two victims. We all know what needs doing here. We have very little to go on so far with this Tell character, but there has to be a thread, something that ties them together, so you four head on down, and you four try to find a link, go on, let's see if we can't catch this guy."

William Tell

Chapter Thirteen

11:28 AM

Tommy, Doreen, Joe, and Therese arrived at the Herald building and met with Gil and Robert Blume in the same office where they had held their previous meeting. They all took a seat, and Gil, wearing latex gloves, placed the new William Tell letter and the envelope in front of Tommy, along with a copy, of which additional copies were handed out to the rest of the task force.

ANOTHER BITCH BITES THE DUST!!

HELLO NEW YORK CITY, I KING INCEL,
WILLIAM TELL HAVE STRUCK AGAIN!

MY LIST IS FAR FROM COMPLETED
SO YOU CAN EXPECT MORE TO COME!!

IN FACT MY LIST IS GROWING, AND
PROBABLY WILL CONTINUE, AS THERE
IS NO SHORTAGE OF RUDE BITCHES
IN THIS CITY!!

AND THE INEPTITUDE OF THE NYPD
IS MAKING IT SO EASY!!
IS IT THREE NOW?
HOW MANY MORE TO GO???
WHY MUST I CONTINUE???

STAY TUNED, I'M COMING FOR MORE!

Everyone read the letter and sat for a moment taking it in, then Tommy asked; "What's an incel? He calls himself King Incel here, but I don't know what he's talking about?"

"It's…" Both Doreen and Gil began to answer at the same time. "Please, Detective, go ahead," Gil said as he gave the room to Doreen.

"Thanks, it's a man who basically has given up on having sex."

"Correct," Joe Hanrahan continued, "It's most always a man, and usually a heterosexual man who not only has given up on having sex but blames women and society for their sexless lives. Incel is short for involuntarily celibate, it's a term used mostly on the internet by millennials and is a fast-growing online subculture."

"Sounds like a new age chauvinist/misogynist type of movement?" Tommy asked.

"Exactly," Gil replied as Joe also nodded in agreement.

"So, we can guess, or assume, that our perp Mr. Tell may possibly be on the younger side of our twenty-five-thirty-five age window, and should most likely be active on the internet?"

"Yup," Doreen interjected, "I bet he posts on, or is part of some manosphere chat groups on reddit or some other online sites, usually these people are, and I would think him declaring himself King Incel, that we'll most likely find he is part of one of these groups, either before or after we catch up to him."

"Manosphere?" Tommy asked.

"Yeah, the manosphere is any group of websites and blogs and the like that promote masculinity and misogyny while opposing feminism."

"Why have I never heard of this stuff?"

"Cause you're a real man, Tommy," Doreen continued, "You have no problem getting women, and when you're around women, you treat them with dignity and respect. Besides that, you're a fucking dinosaur who doesn't even have a Facebook page, so I don't see you being hip to the online millennial lingo these people use on their reddit pages, or the current online pejoratives they use either."

Tommy cocked his head at Doreen, "I don't know if you're complementing me or insulting me there, Doreen?"

Therese smiled, "She's complimenting you."

Doreen shook her hand slightly and replied, "Eh? A little of both."

Robert Blume then stated, "We'll run this letter in the next edition, same as we did with the last. Do a simple piece about the case as a whole. Can we get any input from you detectives on what is happening on your end?"

The four of them stayed quiet for a moment, their eyes quickly darting back and forth from one another's, then Joe spoke up.

"You can write down that the detectives of the William Tell Task Force had no comment to give at the time, but did confirm that they were following up on several different leads and forensic evidence and intend to have William Tell in custody soon." He paused, then said, "And you can go ahead and put my name to that if you have to?"

Blume then asked, "What do you have, Detective?"

"Very little, sir. The truth is, despite the hours put in by Detectives Keane and Doyle and the rest of our team as a whole, we have very little. William Tell is either quite intelligent and wily, or the luckiest fucker in the city, so far, his crime scenes have been left practically clueless, zero evidence outside of the bolts he's left behind, no forensics to speak of as of yet. We also have yet to find a single link between any of our victims, so no, right now with three, or possibly more victims down, we, to be honest, have nothing to run with at the moment."

"Possibly more?" Gil asked, and all heads turned towards Joe.

"I may be reading into this a bit, but read the sixth line in his letter… "IS IT THREE DOWN NOW?"

"You think there's another dead girl, and he's taunting us?" Tommy asked.

"Or playing a game, trying to throw us off track. Either way, I think this is an intelligent guy. Crazy? Absolutely, but intelligent, and he put that in there for a reason, either to taunt us or to push us in a different direction or maybe just to get a thrill by adding a little more terror to his story and scaring the shit out of the city wondering if there may be more?"

Joe paused, and everyone pondered what he had just said. He then continued, "But regardless of what this guy wrote in this letter, at the moment we have little to go on right now,

Mr. Blume, but we will have him in custody soon, that I can promise you, and I can be sure of this because we have a first-rate crew working on this, and there will absolutely be a break in this case that will expose this man, and when we get it we will have him, it's just a matter of time. Unfortunately, it's the one thing we have so very little to spare."

They ended their meeting with that. Tommy had Gil place the letter and envelope into a brown paper evidence bag after the rest of the team had taken a good look at it and later sent it off to the lab for analysis.

And they all returned to the precinct.

***

3:02 PM

As the task force members who had visited the Herald building filed their way back into their cramped office, Miguel leaned back in his chair next to his desk and with a big smile on his face, announced that he had found a connection via the video tapes he had been examining since the task force was formed.

Miguel, was exceptionally proficient when it came to reviewing the sometimes hundreds even thousands of hours of video captured during different investigations, a knack he believed he garnered from the hours and hours of television he and his sister watched growing up in the projects with a strict mother who rarely let them out of her site, much less to run around in the streets like other neighborhood kids.

Miguel was the one always to point out mistakes, plot holes, microphones, mismatched clothing items, any inconsistencies he could find in the programs he and his sister would spend hours watching, then later in life, during his career as an NYPD Detective he found a way to put this somewhat questionable talent to work, and became known as "The Critic" by some of his fellow detectives, because of his critical abilities regarding movies and television, but more so for his ability to see the unseen on closed circuit video.

"What you find, Mickey?" Joe asked.

"Here, come take a look, I spliced a couple of pieces together."

The team gathered around his desk as best they could, and then he began to play his edited video on his monitor.

"This is York Avenue, right around the corner from the crime scene, the night of Kaylee Reese's murder. We got this from the deli the next block over. Notice the time, it's about forty minutes before the 911 call, here see this guy, black hood pulled up over his baseball cap, looks like a white male, beard, possible glasses, and a black bag… four minutes later he passes by again, then two minutes later again. Okay, now we're up the block from the Asphalt Green, and this is almost five minutes before the 911 call, same guy? I don't know, but it's pretty close. Here he's walking East on 90th away from where Kaylee was killed, then here just for a second, and here he is again, crossing 1st Avenue."

Miguel hit pause, "Unfortunately, this video is all pretty shitty, but wait, I got more!"

Miguel hit play. "Here we are at the Heather Mills murder, the prior week. Nice bright day with excellent lighting. Unfortunately, this video comes from half a block away, and when I enhance it, it gets really grainy, but what do we see here? I'll tell you what, a man, dressed in dark clothing hood up, possibly with a ball cap on, carrying a similar sized black bag, he enters the building, note the time, it's about an hour before the 911 call is placed, here he is leaving the building about eighteen minutes before the 911 call is placed.

"I haven't gone over all the Jenna Morrison videos yet, but regardless, I think we have our guy here. It's tough to tell, but he's a light-skinned male. From what little we see, I would say by comparing him to stationary objects as best I can, he's probably shorter than I am, maybe five feet five or five feet six? And just looking at how he moves, I would guess he's a young man who would fit our twenty-five-thirty-five age range."

"Okay, well, we're starting to get a little something on this guy, aren't we?" Tommy began, "Doreen, you want to put together a board for us, I know you like the creative stuff, see what we can put together with these three victims, we'll do a little algebra, a column for each girl, the circumstances, similarities, connections of any sort, anything you can think of, and our X in this problem of course is our King Incel William Tell, we have something? We must have something between the three women that will point us to this savage. Let's see if we can break it down."

"You got it, Tommy."

"Joe, Therese, Miguel, what are we missing, what have I failed to do so far to catch this fucker?

"Honestly, Tommy, I've read every word in these case folders four times now, and I can honestly say I can't see where you failed. Unfortunately, Mathews was the wrong guy for the Mills girl, but not for nothing. He made perfect sense as the perp, and I woulda charged him too," Joe said.

Therese interjected, "The problem here, people, is not what you've done, or what we are now doing, it's that this animal is on a rampage, and here we are with three bodies in less than two weeks. I've never seen or studied a spree quite like this. He's moving so fast, but with intent, and apparently in a particularly methodical manner, we now know he has a list, which scares the fucking shit out of me, but he also is fucking up."

"How?" Jimmy asked.

"He's bringing attention to himself. Yes, he wants to kill these women, but he craves the attention and the notoriety more. We're going to catch him, no doubt in my mind. My hope is that we do before he strikes again."

Therese paused, then continued.

"In many ways he's showing us that he doesn't just want to kill these girls, he wants credit for killing these girls, he wants notoriety, he wants to be caught, to be a hero to other twisted fucks, what was it he said – "All the greats are eventually caught?" He went to the press to have his letters published; he is so far remaining in this small geographic area of only about a mile; he's not running; he's here, and I bet you anything he knows these women."

William Tell

Chapter Fourteen

It was midnight before the team called it quits for the night, fourteen hours in and maybe an inch closer to finding their killer.

Tommy stepped onto the sidewalk outside the precinct and breathed the cool night air deeply. 'Ten hours,' he thought, 'Ten hours and I'll be back here."

He pulled out his phone and texted Molly, 'You home, Molly? You up still?'

As he crossed Third Avenue, he received a reply, 'Yeah, I'm up, I'm home. What's up? Do you want to come over?'

'Yes, I would, Molly, but I don't want to fool around tonight. I just want to get some sleep, but not sleep alone if that's ok?'

'Of course, come over, please. I miss you.'

'Be there in thirty.'

Tommy walked the eighteen or so blocks to Molly's apartment, trying hard to clear his head and fall into that self-meditative state he could when he needed to empty his mind. Still, he was finding it impossible to do so, the lack of sleep, and the stress of knowing this killer was out there on the very streets he was walking, looking to cross another girl off his list, was unbearable. He had investigated dozens of homicide cases, but this one was different, different because the perpetrator was waiting in the dark, stalking his next victim. Tommy knew he was helpless; as of that moment, he knew there was nothing he could do to keep this individual from striking again, and it ate at his soul.

***

Tommy walked up the steps of Molly's building, rang the bell, and waited for her to buzz him in. Then, he went up the stairs to her door and softly knocked.

"Tommy?" Molly asked.

"Yeah, it's me."

"Okay, prepare yourself." She said as the locks tumbled open, one, two, three.

"Prepare myself? Listen, Molly…"

Molly stood in front of Tommy in the short Yankee jersey she had worn for all of three minutes on their first night together. It took him a second to realize and then for his face to react.

"Do you hate it?" She asked, "I wanted to do something. It just seemed smart. I don't know. You hate it, don't you?"

He smiled and shook his head, "No, I don't hate it at all."

Molly had cut her hair into a short bob cut with sharp bangs and dyed it jet black, except for a thin red stripe that ran down the left side of her face.

"I had my friend Donna over at the salon do it. Meghan and I both went. This William Tell killer seems to like girls with long blonde hair, so we thought it was smart to change our looks. You know, for safety, so, do you hate it?"

"Molly, you sweet thing. No, I think it was a smart move, and… there is absolutely nothing I hate about you, nothing at all."

She threw her arms around Tommy and hugged him with all her might. Then she kissed him.

"Are you sure you don't want to fool around? It'll be like cheating on me, only with me?" She said with a big smile and a playful voice, excited to see Tommy again and happy he didn't hate her new look.

"No, honey, I really need to sleep. Let me just take a shower, and then we can get to bed, okay?"

Molly pursed her lips, looking sorrowful. "Can I join you in the shower?"

"No, I'm sorry, honey. Please just let me get cleaned up, and then we can go to bed tonight, okay?"

"Okay, " she replied, halfway pouty in an attempt to be cute but also slightly concerned. She had never seen Tommy so beat before, and that worried her.

William Tell

After his shower, Tommy set his phone alarm for 8:30, which would give him just over 7 hours if he were to fall asleep quickly. Once he lay in bed and put his arm around Molly's warm naked body, that's precisely what happened. Tommy was out within minutes.

***

Tommy's eyes snapped open, and the early morning light was just entering Molly's bedroom through her lace curtains. Something wasn't right, and it took a second to realize just what. Then, as he lay on his back in her bedroom, he realized that everything was actually more than right.

He knew what was happening, and as he looked down to confirm it, he could see the bedspread move up and down in a slow and steady motion as Molly rhythmically worked Tommy's erection with her mouth and hand from under the covers.

"Molly, you are so fresh, but you sure know how to wake a fella up, don't you?"

"Are you awake now, lover?" She asked, still under the blankets; she then ran her tongue up Tommy's belly, then chest, neck, and chin before sitting up and inserting him into herself with a soft gasp. "Ooh," She said softly but dramatically for effect, "I have missed you. I have missed you so much these last few days, my sweet, sexy man."

"And I have missed you."

"Really, how about now? Do you miss the old me, or does the new goth-haired me turn you on?"

Tommy laughed, "I liked you just the way you were, kid, but if the new you keeps waking me up this way, I think the new you may just be an improvement."

Molly gave Tommy a light, playful slap across the face, "You're calling me fresh? That was fresh!"

Tommy smiled and then grabbed Molly by the hips, flipping her over onto her back where he began to ride her with the steady rhythm he knew she loved. He continued until her body began to tighten with ecstasy. They both finished, exhaling with the joy and satisfaction they had come to love so much from one another.

William Tell

Chapter Fifteen

10:02 AM

Tommy walked into the Task Force office a new man. After seven hours of sleep and a remarkably satisfying morning behind him, he was ready to dig back into this case. As he crossed the threshold, he found Doreen, who was just finishing up a board where she had laid out all their work so far.

The first column had a photo of their first victim, Heather Mills, with everything they knew about her listed under it. Then, a second column with Kaylee Reese and then Jenna Morrison. At the end of the board, about 20 inches past Jenna's photo, was a single piece of paper with a large black X in the middle of it to represent the X of their algebra problem.

Tommy paused as he looked at it. Each column with each victim had brief notes on what they knew about each of the girls who were killed, and there were a couple of notes under the X as well. He stared at it until Doreen spoke up.

"What? What? You don't like it? What's the matter with it?"

"No, it's, it's nothing, Doreen." Tommy looked as if he were getting choked up a bit.

Doreen asked in a softer voice, "What's up? What's bothering you?"

Tommy ran his finger across his mouth and took a deep breath. "I'm Sorry. It's great. You did great."

"No, what? What is it?"

"I just, it's the space, it just threw me for a second, I'm sorry."

"The space? What are you talking about?"

Tommy leaned over and ran his finger across the board, the 20 or so inches from Jenna Morrison's photo to the paper with the X on it, then, with a tear welling up in his eye, said,

"There will be more. I'm afraid there will be more, and we will have to fill this space with their photos."

"Oh no, no, Tommy, I apologize, I didn't mean to…"

"No, stop. You didn't do anything wrong, this is great, you did a great job, it just hit me hard, that's all, don't, don't be silly, this is exactly what I was asking for, just seeing it laid out kinda hooked me, that's all, I'm sorry… It's been a long couple of weeks."

Again, it was only the second day after Jenna Morrison's murder, and every member of the team was in for the day. Tommy, the lead detective on this case, ran a little meeting while everyone was together to reboot the case as a whole.

"So, here we are with another victim, another letter, a panicked city, the press up our ass, and the brass and mayor's office even further up our asses wanting us to catch this creep… I'm sure we all know this, but let me emphasize it, we're doing exactly everything we're supposed to be doing, and we absolutely will catch this guy, we just have to keep going: slowly, methodically, paying attention to every detail, and then, yes, going over it all again."

Tommy took a breath and continued, "Brenda here has a long and growing list of people who have called in with tips over the last few days. Therese and Jimmy, I think you two should team up and see how much of a dent we can put into that list and see if any of these call-ins pan out."

"Absolutely." Therese said, followed by a "Sure thing." From Jimmy.

"Miguel, you just keep banging away with the surveillance video. You've located what we think is our possible, what, three times now?"

"Four so far, and now that I have an idea what to look for, I know I'll have more soon."

"I know you will, Miguel, and I know I would never find the things you find… Gloria, you keep compiling and cross-referencing all the minutia of these cases. It seems you have a knack for it, keep it up; you know what to do. Give us some spreadsheets on any license plates, parking tickets from the locations and these dates, find out who owns these buildings, are there any cameras we haven't found? Just do your thing and patch together anything that looks like any kind of a pattern or worthwhile clues we can chase after."

"Already ahead of you and on it, Tommy. You know how I roll." Gloria replied.

"Doreen, you are fantastic on the computer, you get to digging into every angle and avenue you can come up with to connect us with our guy, and anything that may connect these girls. We know there has to be a connection. I don't believe these girls are typical random attacks by this guy, I believe they are targeted for a reason, and I really think we will find there is a connection somewhere, and of course keep abreast of, and cross-reference everything Brenda and Gloria find, as well as any and all names Therese and Jimmy are going to interview."

"You got it."

"Joe, you are this team's most senior and experienced person. Sir, please help me conduct this little orchestra we have here. Watch over us all, including me, maybe even especially me. I know you're not afraid to get your hands dirty, and you will, but please watch for any details we may miss. Also, let's arrange it so the two of us have opposite days off, whatever they may be, and make it easy on you, that way either you or I will always have a hand on the rudder."

Joe stood and smiled at Tommy's humility as he stuck his hand out and silently shook Tommy's. Joe was all too familiar with how big cases like these could go to a detective's head or, conversely, have a weaker man hide his head in the sand. Still, with this little pep talk Tommy just gave, he now knew they were being led by a man who was a true detective, and whose only reason for being on the job was to get the bad guys. Though Joe had worked with so many others in his thirty-plus years on the job, these last few minutes, combined with Tommy's reputation, had Joe recognizing Tommy as a man to be admired.

***

After a little more back-and-forth, everyone began working earnestly in their different areas of expertise. As they did, Tommy excused himself, stepped into the stairway, and dialed the number to Reif's Tavern on his cell.

"Reif's, what can I do you for?" A woman answered.

"I need to speak to Terry, please."

"Ain't no Terry here, honey. No one by that name hangs out in here that I know…"

Tommy cut her off, "Listen, this is important. Have someone tell him to call Tommy right away, please."

"I don't know who you are or who you're looking for, but there ain't no Terry here!" The woman said, then hung up.

Tommy then messaged his dear friend Roya Sarhadi, from his mother's building, who had helped him with some computer hacking during the Hayden Jon Marshall and Li Jun cases: 'Hey Roya how you doing? You available for a quick meet sometime today?'

He then sat on the stairs about halfway between the 3rd and 4th floors and relaxed momentarily as he tried to collect his thoughts. He was going to go all out, he didn't know what road would lead to the apprehension of William Tell, but if it took the most brutal most connected criminal in the neighborhood, or some illegal computer hacking to get the job done, well, Tommy knew it wasn't beneath him to go that route, in fact he wondered why he hadn't reached out to Terry already, these streets were both his life and his business after all, and no one knew them better than Terry Calahan.

Two minutes passed before he received a text from Roya: 'Hi Tommy, absolutely, I'm off at 5:00 and completely available today.'

'Great, 6:00 a good time to grab a bite and talk for a bit? You're on your way home, you tell me where.'

'How about Delizia, the pizzeria on 92nd?'

'Perfect, I'll see you there at 6:00.'

Tommy had no idea how or if Roya could help him with this case. He had nothing to share with her to get her started, but he was desperate to end this case. With three bodies and more promised, he thought she would be primed to move if a lead of any kind were to be discovered.

He sat for a few more minutes, then stood and returned to the office.

For the next ninety minutes, he shuffled through the mounting paperwork on the three victims. It seemed to him and the rest of the team that the only link between these women so far was that they were all beautiful blondes in their mid-twenties who lived on the Upper East Side.

"All we know," Joe said, "Is it seems he has a type."

***

Tommy's phone began to buzz; he didn't recognize the number. "Keane." He answered.

"Hey, how you doing? I heard you're lookin for me?" It was Tommy's lifelong friend and underworld figure, Terry Calahan.

Tommy stood up. "Hey, thanks for getting back," he added as he stepped back into the hallway and halfway down the stairs from the office. "You available for a quick get-together?"

"Yeah, of course, I'll need a little bit. Where and what time you thinking?

"I got meeting at six on 2nd Avenue, you wanna do five, and anywhere you like."

"Yeah, five will do, I gotta see a guy on 97th today, how about we do like when Sissy's aunt was in the hospital and meet on the benches outside the park across from Mount Sinai Hospital again?"

"That's perfect, I look forward to it."

The two of them said their goodbyes, and Tommy returned to the office to again read through everything that had been compiled so far, this time making notes of any details he believed Terry or Roya would be interested in.

At 4:00 PM, Tommy told Doreen he was heading out to meet with a CI (confidential informant) he had working the streets and bars for them. He said he would also grab a bite, but should be back before the end of the tour.

William Tell

At 4:48 PM, Tommy sat on a bench against Central Park's stone wall opposite the entrance to Mount Sinai Hospital when he saw Terry and his right-hand man, Gusty Cole, across the avenue on the corner, where they had stopped and conversed. Terry then crossed 5th Avenue alone and made his way over to Tommy. As he did, Tommy made eye contact with Gusty, and both gave one another the obligatory neighborhood nod of recognition.

Terry, dressed in his usual black leather car coat, black crew-neck sweatshirt, blue jeans, and Adidas Superstars, wrapped his arms tightly around Tommy, squeezing him tightly. Their leather jackets crunched and squeaked against one another as they embraced. "Good to see you, brother," Terry said into Tommy's ear before kissing him on the cheek and then releasing him.

"Look at that jacket! It fits you perfectly, man!" Terry said with pride, speaking of the brown leather car coat he had sent to Tommy after the shooting in the Li Jun case had ruined Tommy's old one. "Sorry about the brown, but they were all out of black in your size when Sissy and I went to pick it up, but fuck me if the brown don't look better? Shit, I think I'll pick one up for myself now seeing just how handsome you are in it."

"Hey," Tommy paused, a little embarrassed he hadn't thanked Terry for the gift yet. "Thank you for the jacket, Terry. It was a pleasant surprise."

"Don't mention it, was nothing, I couldn't have you running around the streets with holes in your clothes, and I know you ain't making shit with that cop pay and Caitlyn off in college, so don't mention it... And I'm sorry I never came to visit, I figured, well, you know, you don't need me showing up at the hospital, and then have all the cop bosses asking questions. I get that, let me tell you, you motherfucker, you had me worried though, 'Cop shot in the head' was all over the news… Man you had me scared, but fuck me, that head of yours always was made of concrete, I should have known that chink kids bullet couldn't hurt my boy Tommy… I shoulda known." Terry said the last three words a little softer as a bit of emotion crept out of the complex man's mouth, revealing his love for his dear friend and his sorrow that their life choices and professions now kept them apart.

"So… What you need, Tommy? What can I do for you?"

Tommy paused and looked down at the sidewalk before he spoke. Again, He was ashamed to ask his friend for assistance when he couldn't and wouldn't even share a simple beer with him because of their chosen professions.

"I wanna ask you, if you could, keep an ear out for anything at all related to this William Tell fucker. We're breaking our ass looking for clues but keep coming up empty. We got all kinds of kooks calling in with useless information, even a few confessions, but all bullshit, everything is turning out to be bullshit, and we know he's going to strike again, so…"

Terry cut him off, "Tommy, we're all over this, this motherfucker is a danger to all our women, you don't think everyone has an eye out and an ear to the ground? You kidding me? In fact, he better hope we don't find his ass before you do, cause I got a day full of torture planned for every girl he's killed so far, and that ain't just me, that's every crew in New York.

William Tell, whoever this cunt is, is number one on everybody's priority list. You can take that to the bank."

"I figured as much, but please do me a favor. Let's pass on the torture and murder if you can, and if you get a lead, just give me a call."

Tommy handed Terry a sheet of paper from his memo book with a description of what they believed William Tell may look like from the little video they had pieced together: Light-skinned male, Mid-Late 20s, Beard, all-black clothing, Hoodie, Ball Cap, Glasses, carrying a bag: 15-20 inches long by 12-15 inches wide.

"Not much here, is there? And no promises on the killing or torturing, but if I get any leads or any info at all, I'll absolutely give you a call."

"Thanks, brother. I appreciate it," Tommy followed up with, as he gave Terry a firm handshake and a tight hug, "Give my love to Sissy please – and hey, how's Gusty doing?"

"I will; she misses you, you know, she always liked you. And Gusty? Well, he's the same as he ever was, eats too much, drinks too much, and sleeps too much, but the fucker is there whenever I need him… He's a good friend. No Tommy Keane, of course, but he's a good friend."

Terry walked back across the Avenue, and he and Gusty headed north towards 97th Street. Tommy then headed down to 92nd and 2nd for his meeting with Roya.

***

5:44 1762 2nd Avenue, Delizia Restaurant and Pizzeria.

Tommy arrived a little early and leaned against a car outside the pizzeria, watching the people pass by, trying to remember how many hundreds of times he had eaten there over the years.

Delizia opened in 1988 at this location; they had another spot on 73rd that was even older. Both did an excellent job, and Tommy was happy Roya had chosen this place. He hadn't visited for a few years and was a little excited to return.

He smiled as he noticed Roya walking down the block in her black skinny jeans, black Converse, a maroon nylon flight jacket, and a knit cap with cat ears sticking up on either side of her head. Her long black hair bouncing out from under it as she approached him.

"Hey," she said as she got closer and gave him a hug. "New coat? I like it!" she said as she stepped back and ran her hands down the front of it, feeling the luxury of the fine leather. They then headed into the restaurant.

Delizia was a classic old-school New York City Pizzeria in the front, with a slightly more formal dining room at the back. It had a welcome feeling with exposed brick, white cloth tablecloths, and napkins; this is where Tommy and Roya took a seat. The waitress, a small Italian woman of about fifty-five, immediately took their order. Knowing what she wanted, Roya asked for the Chicken Francese and Tommy the Chicken Rollatini, then Roya asked.

"So, what's the case this time, Tommy?"

He smiled, "What makes you think I didn't want just to have dinner and visit with you, Roya?"

"I know you too well. If you just wanted to say hello, you would have just come upstairs and knocked on my door. A dinner invite means we have a case that needs to be cracked, and you need help cracking it."

"Man, am I that predictable and easy to read?"

"Like a book, but the answer is yes, just let me know what you need."

"Yes? That was quick, don't you want to at least know…"

"No, if you're reaching out to me, it means you need help, and if you need help, I am here for you. So, what can I do?"

Tommy smiled. He had loved Roya since she was a little girl, and he was now so proud of the smart, courageous woman she had become.

"Okay Roya, well in this case I don't know what I need or if or how you may be able to assist me, but it's this William Tell fucker. We have three dead girls, all about your age, and almost zero to go on. I have no idea what to do with this one, Roya. So far, his crime scenes are spotless, we can't find a link between the girls, I'm sure you know he's now writing into the papers to play with us, and… And he says there will be more. He says he has a list and there will be more victims, and here I am, I have a team of six detectives, all top-notch investigators, and so far, nothing, not a fucking thing to run with. I don't know what you can do, but if there are any high-speed computer dragnets you can throw out there and maybe catch a hint of something, I'd love you to try, kid."

"Hmmm," Roya hummed as she thought for a moment, "It will be tough to search with nothing to go on, but I can certainly run the victims social media and emails addresses for links and patterns, maybe find something there, and of course anything new that comes through you can pass on to me and we'll, well we'll just run with anything and everything we can and see what interests you?"

"My thoughts exactly. I know I have very little for you to start with, but if we can get some sort of search started and just add to it, who knows, we may just stumble across something pertinent."

"Exactly. Give me what you have, and we'll get something up and running tonight."

Tommy gave her all the victims' information he had, dates of birth, social security numbers, email addresses, and any social media he knew they used, absolutely everything he had; he handed it over to Roya. Then, once everything was handed over and a course of action decided upon, they returned to their meals. They chatted about one another's lives for about an hour before Roya headed home to plug all of this information into her computers, and Tommy went back to the precinct for more investigations and to sign out for the evening.

William Tell

Chapter Sixteen

The next few days dragged on with little progress in the investigations. The team, along with Captain Pileggi and Lieutenant Bricks, conducted two separate press conferences, where they sheepishly said nothing more than "We're doing everything we can at the moment, and are happy with the intelligence and progress we have made in the William Tell case thus far." Then deflected every question posed by the press. This was nothing but lies, of course. Captain Pileggi had no choice but to lie and give false hope to a City that was riddled with fear in an attempt to keep its residents calm. But the reality was that the William Tell Task Force was no closer to closing this case than they were the night of Heather Mill's murder.

So far, Tommy's attempts at reaching out outside of his team, onto the streets through Terry Calahan, and out into the cyberworld through Roya had also turned up nothing.

The sixty-eight interviews conducted during this week's investigations of people who had called in with possible leads or outright confessions proved fruitless and erroneous.

As Tommy sat in the Task Force office, staring up at photos of the victims, with Doreen and Gloria typing away on their computers, Miguel watching surveillance videos as he chewed on a turkey sandwich, and Therese thumbing through the files that were growing daily on these cases desperately looking for a link, Tommy's phone went off. He could see it was Gil Nunez.

"Hey, Gil, how you doing?"

"We just received a new letter, Tommy, can you make it down?"

"I'll be there in less than thirty." And then he hung up the phone, stood, and grabbed his jacket.

"That was Gil Nunez; The Herald just got a new letter. Doreen, Therese, you wanna join me?"

Both women stood and grabbed their jackets, neither saying a word. The whole team was becoming overwhelmed and somber over the case, not by its workload, but by its stagnation, lack of evidence, and most of all by the impending doom of the promise of more to come.

The three detectives walked into the meeting room, where they sat down with Gil and Robert Blume. The letter was on the table, with the envelope right next to it.

Blume didn't bother to welcome the detectives; he just began speaking.

"Here it is, and in this one he mentions you by name, Keane."

ANOTHER BITCH IS ON THE WAY
NEW YORK
AND MY LIST IS GROWING!!

DETECTIVE KEANE IS ON THE CASE
CURIOUS WHAT HE IS KNOWING??

YOU MAY THINK ME EVIL
YOU MAY THINK ME MEAN —
DID YOU THINK I WOULD BE SO
CLEVER AND SO CLEAN??

TRUTH IS IT'S THESE BITCHES
WHO WERE MEAN, AND THEY ALL
GOT WHAT THEY ASKED FOR!!

SO WHAT COMES NEXT??

MORE MORE MORE!!

Tommy, Doreen, and Therese all read and examined the letter closely. Then, Tommy donned latex gloves, placed the letter and its envelope into a brown paper evidence bag, and sealed it.

"He's mentioning you by name, Keane, obviously to taunt you. Maybe to rile you and throw you off track a bit? Maybe just for fun? What do you think?" Robert Blume asked. His hands clasped and resting across his overly huge belly.

Tommy paused. He didn't know what to think and didn't want to say anything that the paper might quote.

"I don't have any comment on this letter or William Tell's frame of mind when writing it. All I can say is that we have several leads we are currently investigating. We believe an arrest is imminent." Tommy felt every bit the lying politician he thought Captain Pillegi, or the mayor, was, but at the same time, what could he say to the press and the city? That he had nothing?

Blume and Gil looked at Tommy. They stared for a moment. Both could see he was at a loss, tired, not quite beaten or broken, but definitely on his way to be. Their eyes shifted to Doreen and Therese, both of whom looked as though they hadn't gotten much sleep over the last couple of weeks. Both also carried that look of worry and guilt that they knew they had nothing.

Chapter Seventeen

Day 16 2:56 AM

Tommy's eyes snapped open in the darkness of his room at his mother's apartment on 88th Street. His phone buzzed on the nightstand. He picked it up and saw the time, 02:56. He didn't recognize the number.

"Oh god, what now?" he said aloud, and as he did, little JoJo snapped to attention and hopped onto Tommy's chest. "Not now, boy!" Tommy said sternly and pushed the little dog off him. "Keane," he said, answering the phone.

"Detective Keane, sorry it's so late. Detective Ryan here, Nightwatch. It looks like you have another William Tell killing."

"Where? Where is it? I'll be right over."

"19th between 2nd and 3rd, how long you think?"

"This time of the morning, on a weekday? Hopefully, I can be there in half an hour."

"Okay, great. Neither Crime Scene nor the ME has arrived yet. See you soon, buddy, and again, I'm sorry."

Tommy got up and got dressed. He didn't bother to shower or shave; he just wanted to move quickly and get downtown as soon as possible.

***

3:34 AM

Tommy exited a cab on the northwest corner of 2nd Avenue and 19th Street, where he found several patrol cars, and the block taped off with police tape. He identified himself and walked a little less than halfway up the block, where he could see a group of detectives and uniformed officers standing around the body of a young blonde-haired woman.

"Keane, how are you? Ryan, Dennis Ryan, good to know you, and sorry again for the early morning call, but, well, here you go. You can see why for yourself."

Tommy shook Detective Ryan's hand but solemnly kept his eyes focused on the corpse.

The blonde lay face down on the sidewalk, her head tilted slightly to the left, enough to see one open green eye staring at nothing. She was another beauty, an exceptionally attractive young woman who, like the others, appeared to be in her mid-twenties.

A crossbow bolt with a red flight, precisely the same as the others, was sunk deep into the back of her neck just above her shoulders, and a second bolt stuck out of her back just below her left shoulder blade.

"Do we know anything about her yet?" Tommy asked.

"No, nothing. We haven't touched a thing. Patrol got the call and arrived. We showed up just a few minutes later. Crime Scene has been notified, and the Medical Examiner has been notified as well. Both are en route and should be here soon," Ryan replied.

Tommy squatted down next to the body and studied it for about two minutes, then stood up and slowly moved back to take in a larger view, moving around the corpse to take in every angle.

"No witnesses, I assume?"

"No, not yet."

"And who called it in, do we know?"

"Yes, that gentleman across the street with the white dog on the stoop." He nodded toward the building where a man was sitting with his head down, "Says he didn't see the attack, just saw the body lying on the sidewalk from his window on the third floor, then came down with his dog to investigate… then seeing what we see here, he called 911."

Tommy's eyes were still locked on his new victim's body as Detective Ryan finished his answer to the question. Tommy turned and made his way across the street where a reasonably large, heavyset, dark-skinned balding man with a salt and pepper beard, wearing blue pajamas and a plaid bathrobe sat with a small fluffy white dog on his lap, watching intently past the uniformed officer who stood to the right of him, at the crime scene he had called in less than an hour ago.

"Hello, sir…" Tommy began but was promptly cut off by the gentleman in the bathrobe.

"Detective Thomas Keane, I presume?"

"Yes, sir, Detective Keane, 21st Precinct."

"I assumed it would be you. Your name and your reputation precede you, Detective… I am Robert Clemson the 3rd, and as I am sure you know, I am the individual who made the 911 call that brings us together at this very early hour of the morning." Robert Clemson spoke smoothly and eloquently, something that immediately captivated Tommy.

"Please, tell me what you saw and what you know."

"I was up; nothing unusual for me there, detective, I am both a bit of an insomniac and a night owl. I was watching television and got up to refill my glass with a little chardonnay I had been sipping, and as I returned to my seat, I noticed what appeared to be that young woman's legs from my vantage point above. All I could see were her legs and feet lying on the sidewalk between the two parked cars, and from where I was looking, she didn't appear to be a homeless vagrant, not with those high-heeled shoes and clean dungarees."

"So, nothing drew you to the window, sir? You didn't hear or see anything that made you look out your window."

"No, Detective, I believe I know why you're asking. Sadly no, I, unfortunately, did not witness the attack itself, just the heartbreaking aftermath; again as I sat my glass down on my side table, this young woman's legs caught the corner of my eye as something unusual, so I put on my robe and put the harness on my dog Bennett here. We came down to see if this woman needed some help. I think I assumed she would possibly have just fallen, possibly had been out drinking, but, well, I never expected to find what I found, Detective Keane."

"You're a good man, Mr. Clemson. Many people would have returned to the TV, not caring enough to render any aid at all."

"Yes, yes, these are troubled, uncaring times we live in, aren't they?"

"Is there anything else you can add, Mr. Clemson? Tommy asked as he handed him his card.

Mr. Clemson took the card and paused momentarily; taking in a breath, he answered in a much less eloquent manner, "Catch this evil motherfucker Detective, and if he gives you any opportunity, any opportunity at all, shoot him dead."

Tommy pursed his lips and lowered his head in somber recognition of Mr. Clemson's least eloquent but most damning words of the morning.

As their conversation ended and Mr. Clemson rose from his seat on the stoop, Tommy heard the Crime Scene van pull up the block. The two shook hands, then parted ways, and Tommy returned to the beautiful young corpse waiting for him across the street.

While Crime Scene took their measurements, photographs, and swabs, searching for the minutest of clues, Tommy silently stood and watched, taking in everything he could. Soon, ME Angela Marcus, aka "The Vampire" from the medical examiner's office, joined him. Angela, as always, was overdressed for her job; she wore a ¾ length black leather double-breasted coat over a bright yellow pant suit with black patent leather pumps, and her short blonde hair and make-up were, of course, perfect; she slowly and gently scratched her chin with her perfectly French manicured nails.

"This is number four, isn't it, Keane?" she asked, standing right next to him, looking down at the body while the crime scene detectives fluttered around it.

Tommy slowly nodded, still staring at the body, "Yes, it is."

Tommy was exhausted, not just physically but mentally, and now, with this fourth girl lying just feet away from them on the cold concrete and the recent letters from what they believed most certainly was the actual perpetrator of these awful acts showing up, he began to feel a bit like a victim himself.

A helpless guilt began stabbing at his soul, the helplessness that this may happen again, and the guilt that if only he had caught this murderous bastard after the Heather Mills murder, Kaylee Reese, Jenna Morrison, and this new young woman would all still be alive, and completely unaware they were ever even targeted.

"Listen, Keane, the cause of death is pretty obvious here. Let's forget the protocol for this one, and don't bother making it down for the autopsy. It will be a waste of valuable time. You'll get a full report, and if I find anything unusual at all, I'll call you immediately. But spending time coming to visit me for this one is time you can spend catching this animal, so…"

"Thanks, Angela," Tommy cut her off and said nothing more. They both understood one another, and both just wanted these killings to stop, so they continued their morning in almost complete silence.

As ME. Marcus finished up, Doreen, Jimmy, Therese, and Lieutenant Bricks made the scene, and then, after some brief and somber hellos, they began to search this new victim's body.

Again, as with the others, nothing appeared to be stolen. Tommy recovered her identification and credit cards in a small leather clutch purse tucked inside her jacket pocket. "Madison O'Neil, " he said aloud for all to hear. "Madison O'Neil lives right around the corner on 3rd Avenue; it looks like she was headed home. She is twenty-seven years old and has a school ID here from Hunter College."

"Another beauty," Doreen said as she squatted next to the body, taking in the scene, "Whoever this guy is, he certainly hates the good-looking ones, doesn't he?"

***

The team and a few patrol officers walked through the preliminary on-scene investigation just as they did every other one. All in all, they spent almost four hours at the scene, canvassing the closest buildings, waking people up to do interviews, searching for camera locations, looking through trash cans and the like before calling it quits, and Tommy and

Therese headed over to Madison O'Neil's apartment on 3rd Avenue.

Tommy and Therese looked up at the simple old red brick building, which on the ground level housed a small, currently closed taqueria.

Tommy rang the bell, which read Murphy & O'Neil. They waited a minute, then rang it again. A woman's voice answered the intercom, "Who is it?"

Tommy answered, "Police, ma'am, Detectives from the 21st police precinct, open up, please."

The door lock buzzed, and Tommy and Therese entered the building and went up to the second-floor apartment. Before Tommy could knock, they heard,

"Can you put your badges up to the peephole for me, please?"

Tommy and Therese did as they were asked, and then the locks began to tumble, and the door was cracked open. A short woman with hazel eyes and sandy blonde hair, about twenty-five, eyed the detectives through the crack, the chain still secured.

"Can I see them again, please, and…" She paused, not completing her sentence. She looked again at the Detectives' shields they held up for her and eyed them up and down until she was convinced they were indeed police detectives. Then she undid the chain and opened the door,

"What happened to Madison? That's why you're here, isn't it?" the young twenty-five-year-old Audra Murphy asked. "Something's wrong; she should have been home hours ago, but she's not, and that's why you're here, am I right?"

"I'm sorry to say, yes, you are dear," Tommy said as gently as he could.

"Oh my god, no! What happened? What happened to Madison?" she shrieked.

Therese stepped inside the doorway and placed her hands on the young woman's arms, "Madison is no longer with us, dear. I'm sorry she was killed a few hours ago."

"No! No, no, no, no! This can't be real, what? Who?"

"Come inside and take a seat, please," Therese said as she walked toward a round oak table and chairs in the small apartment's kitchen.

The young woman listened and sat. Therese pulled out one of the other chairs from the dinette set and sat facing her. "What is your name, dear?"

"Audra, Audra Murphy."

"And what is your and Madison's relationship?"

"She's my sister." Just then, her tears began. "Oh my god!" she cried out. "I knew something was wrong."

Therese reached over a violin on the table and took a napkin from its holder, handing it to Audra to wipe the tears from her eyes. Audra began to sob, and Therese moved closer, placing her hand on Audra's shoulder. Taking a couple more napkins from their holder, she gently patted Audra's cheeks to comfort her.

William Tell

It took Audra a moment to calm down and relax enough to be interviewed. When they were done, Tommy and Therese learned that their newest victim, Madison O'Neal, and her younger half-sister, Audra Murphy, had grown up in Sunnyside, Queens. They had moved to Manhattan together almost three years before. Both worked at different restaurants and bars to earn a living. Audra sorrowfully admitted that her beloved Madison would occasionally go on dates as an escort.

When Therese asked if she would have sex with the men on these dates, Audra hung her head and said, "Yes, but not always. Sometimes they were just dates, you know, businessmen who needed an escort for business dinners, men who wanted a classy, beautiful girl on their arm."

"Well, she certainly was a classy and beautiful woman, wasn't she?" Therese replied, in as kind a voice as she could.

They spoke with Audra for about an hour and a half, then looked through Madison's room and belongings in search of any clues they may find. In doing so, they got a good look at Madison's life. She and Audra had grown up together in Sunnyside with their mother, Kim, who worked as a clerk at Metropolitan Hospital before moving to Florida a few years ago with her new husband.

Both girls had graduated from Holy Cross High School, both had some college, and Madison had recently begun taking psych classes at Hunter College. Both girls were also musicians: Madison played the violin, and Audra the harp. Both were also hard workers, waiting tables and tending bar in a handful of different businesses in the city. Neither had serious boyfriends at the moment. Still, both did casually date different men, somewhat sporadically.

Audra said there was no drug use between them other than marijuana and alcohol, and when asked again about the escort jobs, she sheepishly answered.

"My sister, she was so beautiful, and men would ask her out every day. When another woman approached her to do this kind of work, at first she said no, but then went for it when offered a no sex date where she was paid five hundred dollars. Five hundred dollars to go to a banquet for a few hours and fawn over some rich businessman who wanted to look good in front of his clients. Next thing you know, she was doing this four, five, six times a month, and one day she said a date offered her a thousand to come back to his room with him, and she did."

Audra paused, breathed, and wiped the tears from her eyes.

"My sister wasn't a whore, I want you to know that, yes, yes she did, oh my god she did sell herself, but only when she thought the client was hot, and when he offered. It wasn't a regular thing, just, well, I don't know, she just did what she did when she wanted to, and was well paid for it."

"Nobody's judging anybody, Audra," Therese said softly. "We just need to know everything we can to find out who did this to her."

"Thank you," Audra replied. "Thank you both," she said again, looking up at Tommy this time.

Tommy asked, "Can you think of anyone who would want to hurt your sister for any reason? Has she discussed anything or anyone recently or in the past who might have wanted to hurt her?"

"No, no one, everybody loved Madison."

"Were there any guys from the bars or restaurants that may have followed her home, you know, any guys creepin' around her or stalking her?"

"Oh, jeese, Detective, that was an occupational hazard for us, especially for Madison. I mean, every day, waiting or bartending, you have guys hitting on us, you know? Or following us around when we're walking to work or home, but no, I have to say, no one comes to mind right away that I know of and can say needs investigating."

Tommy knelt on the floor next to the chair Audra was sitting in. He placed his hand on her forearm and looked into her hazel eyes, "Audra, your sister Madison was killed by the William Tell killer."

"Oh my god," She gasped.

"And I believe she was targeted, we don't think this was a random attack, we think William Tell is intentionally targeting his victims, so please, I know this is an awful lot to take in this morning, but if you think of anyone, anyone at all, or any incident at all your sister may have told you about, please do not hesitate, give me a call immediately so we can look into it."

"I, I will, Detective Keane, I promise I will."

***

Tommy and Therese then waited for Audra to shower and dress and then took her to the City Morgue, where they walked her in and waited next to the glass viewing window for the tech to roll up the stainless-steal table Madison was laid out on and then for him to remove the sheet that covered her down to her shoulders so Audra could see her sister's face and positively identify her.

Audra placed her palms on the glass and cried aloud as she nodded up and down, saying, "Yes, that's my sister Madison." Through her tears, then directing her attention through the glass to Madison, she screamed, "I love you, Madison! I love you!"

William Tell

Chapter Eighteen

Tommy heard the song Troublemaker by The Fantastic Plastics start with its rhythmic electro beat. As he reached for his phone, he accidentally knocked it onto the floor from the nightstand of his room in his mother's apartment.

"Fuck me." He said under his breath at the thought of having to get up for another day of work, and no sooner did the words leave his lips than his little dog gave him a big wet kiss with his warm tongue right across those very same lips.

"Oh, come on now!" Tommy exclaimed a little louder, not happy to receive his dog's wet affections so early in the morning. Of course, saying anything got JoJo even more excited and had him hopping up and down in the bed in anticipation of Tommy rising and taking him for a walk.

As JoJo pawed and licked him, Tommy sat up in the darkness and pushed the pup away. Then he rolled onto the floor for his fifty morning push-ups, but instead, he lay there, face down, on the cool hardwood as he felt his bones slowly sink down in his body, as if they wanted to embed themselves into the floor and become one with the old oak beneath him.

William Tell

Tommy was exhausted. He hadn't had a decent night's sleep since the seven hours he caught with Molly several nights before, and had had over a week's worth of sleepless nights the week before that. This sleep deficit, combined with the stress of this case, was beginning to really take a toll on him, and as he lay on the cool floor, he decided to skip his morning fifty and settle for the one it took to get him off the floor and back on his feet. It was 8:00 AM, and he needed to get himself together and walk little JoJo, so that's exactly what he did.

As he stepped out of the bedroom on his way to the bathroom, his mother Maria, cigarette hanging out of her mouth as she poured herself her second cup of coffee, said,

"Tommy, you look like shit, have you been sleeping and eating properly, Tommy? You're not drinking too much, are you?"

He squinted from the light in the room as he looked at his mother. Then he slowly looked down at the floor, and as he went to the bathroom, he lowly said, "Drinking too much? I wish I were drinking too much."

He showered and dressed, and as he made his way out of his room and grabbed JoJo's leash from the basket on the counter, his mother asked, "Hey Tommy, you want to know what I think, Tommy?"

"What you think? Of course, Ma, I always want to know your thoughts, but what exactly are we talking about here?"

"Your killer Tommy, your serial killer William Tell, what that's been killing all these girls all around the city Tommy, I been watchin all about it on the television here and reading all about it in the papers Tommy, also was discussing it with Bridey and the girls at mass Tommy."

He paused for a moment and replied, "Of course, Ma. Please tell me what you think."

"I think you're gonna catch him soon, Tommy, because I know you are the best. And I will bet you, I will bet you dollars to doughnuts when you do, he's gonna be a skinny little nothin of a man with zero personality, who couldn't get laid on a dare," Tommy smiled when she said that as he wasn't expecting those words to come out of her mouth, "And that's why he hates women, especially all these beautiful young girls, cause they won't give him the time of day Tommy, you see he hates himself, but takes it out on them."

"Ma, I think you will win that bet, and I hope you're right about us catching him soon."

"Oh, I am Tommy, you'll catch him soon, I know you will, Tommy, I know you will."

Tommy smiled and kissed his mother on the head, then he took JoJo for a quick walk, returned home, and kissed his mother on the head again as she sat in front of the television and lit up her third cigarette of the day, then headed out the door.

Stepping out onto the stoop, he looked to his left and right, scanning the block, then stepped onto the sidewalk and made his way to work.

As he approached the precinct, he could see a crowd of over two dozen people in front of the building within some police line barriers holding signs in protest of something. As he got closer, he could read them.

"Save Our Girls!" "Stop The Killings," "William Tell Must Go To Hell," and "The NYPD Hates Women" were just a few.

As he entered the front door, the two officers standing outside monitoring the protest nodded to him. Sergeant Ruffalo raised his eyebrows and shook his head at Tommy as he walked past the desk to express his disbelief at what Tommy had just seen outside.

***

A little more than an hour had passed, and Tommy, Jimmy, Miguel, and Brenda were all sitting in their tiny office working on various aspects and angles of the case when Tommy felt his phone go off. It was a number he didn't recognize. "Keane," he answered.

"Tommy, my boy, how you doing?" it was Terry, "Happy to say I might maybe got a lead for you on this serial killer motherfucker if you're still interested?" he said with his usual Terry Calahan sarcasm.

"Really?" Tommy said loudly and with enough excitement that everyone in the office turned their heads towards him. "Where are you?" he asked as he stood and stepped out of the room to speak privately.

"I'm home. You wanna meet at the same spot as last time?"

"Yeah, that'd be perfect. What time works for you?"

"I could head right up there, but how bout we say an hour? 12:15, let's say, would work for you?"

"Yup, that works for me. Very good, then. I'll see you in an hour."

12:08

Tommy arrived at the same bench on 5th Avenue across from Mount Sinai Hospital, where he had met Terry just days before, to find him already sitting there, eating a soft pretzel with mustard and drinking a Pepsi.

"You shoulda waited for me, Terry. I woulda bought you lunch," Tommy said sarcastically.

"Ahh, I shouldn't be eatin this shit, but when I passed the cart over there this pretzel was calling to me, I always liked a tasty soft hot pretzel," Terry replied, as he tore off a tiny bit and tossed it to a pigeon that waited patiently for him on the sidewalk.

He sat on the bench beside his friend. "So, you think you have something?"

"Yeah, maybe?"

"What?"

"There's a super, works a couple of buildings on 90th, 121, and 123, I think, could have that wrong, short guy about five-six, older than you were asking about, about forty, dark hair, similar beard and mustache, name is Simsek, first name is Harry."

As Tommy wrote, Terry took a break, then began again. "Word is he's a real creep. None of the women in the neighborhood like him; they complain about how he stares at them and mumbles undiscernible comments as they walk by." Terry paused momentarily for effect, "But here's the interesting part, something I knew you'd like."

"Yeah, what's that?"

"This guy, he's a hunter, goes to a place upstate and kills deer and shit… with a bow and arrow, word is, he chased some fuckin black kids out of the basement with… are you ready for this, Detective? A fuckin cross bow."

"No shit?"

"No shit, he's only three blocks from the Asphalt Green, and a short walk to every other fuckin victim but the one you just caught down on 19th Street."

As Tommy scribbled in his notepad and Terry leaned back into the stone wall behind him, scanning the block and taking another bite of his pretzel, Tommy asked, "Anything else you think you can add, Terry?"

"Anything else? What the fuck more you need? I gave you the first and last name, guy's description, address, and maybe enough probable cause to get you to go for a warrant? I don't know that might be a bit much to ask, but fuck me, you're the flatfoot, get with the detecting, Detective!"

Tommy smiled, "Thanks, Terry, you are the man."

He then stood up and said, "I'd like to sit with you for a while, but I gotta get cracking on this and see if it pans out at all."

He gave Terry a firm handshake, and Terry stood and hugged Tommy tightly, "I love you, brother."

"And I you, my friend." Tommy turned, and as he walked south, Terry called out, "Tommy!"

Tommy turned, and Terry reached into his pocket and handed him a slip of paper: "Here, this is this creep's phone and social security number."

Tommy smiled and shook his head in disbelief. He was about to ask Terry how he got the social, but he knew he would get some self-important smart-ass answer, so he just smiled at Terry and raised the note above his head like a flag of triumph.

As Tommy left his friend and walked down 5th Avenue towards the precinct, he pulled out his cell and called Jimmy Coletti at the office.

"Hey, Tommy, what's up, man?"

"Listen, I want everyone in the office now to find out everything we can about a guy named Harry Simsek, 121 or 123 East 90th, phone number (212) 555-1989, and social security of 000-23-0505. I'm on my way back, should be there in thirty."

"You got it."

***

Upon arrival at the Task Force office, Tommy found a short stack of printouts on Hamza (Harry) Simsek and numerous questions from the team waiting for him.

"Hey, so do we think this is our guy?" Jimmy excitedly asked.

"I don't know, but we got a tip from an exceptionally reliable source to check him out. You guys find anything?"

"Got a lot!" Jimmy replied.

"Alright, well lay it on me, please."

Jimmy began, "So we ran all the info you gave me over the phone, guy's real name is Hamza Simsek, goes by Harry though. He is the super for both of those addresses you gave me, birth date matches what you have, been arrested twice, once twelve years ago for aggravated harassment of a woman who worked for the same building management company he used to work for, he got fired for that, and another time fifteen years ago for sexual assault in the 3rd degree, plead guilty no jail time."

Brenda then began, "Your man is divorced, owns a house in a place called Olive Bridge, New York, up in the Catskills, he owns a late model Toyota Corolla and an older Ford Ranger Pickup, not much on social media, but he's a hunter. We know that because he says so. We also have photos of him with dead deer he's killed, and the best part is… You wanna tell him, Jimmy?"

"Yes, I do! He's a bow hunter, and you know what else we found out?"

"No, but you're going to tell me, right?"

"Couple years ago, 911 call to his building, he made a citizen's arrest of two teenagers he caught breaking into the basement, he held em for patrol with a crossbow, kids were arrested, and the crossbow was confiscated."

"Very interesting. Anything else?"

Miguel began, "Took a few photos we found on Facebook, cross referenced them with the stats we have on him in the computer, and then tried comparing them to the video we have and it is a possible match, he is listed on our records as about fifteen to twenty pounds heavier than he appears in our video's, but we all know that video isn't always accurate once we pinch a guy, also he could have dropped a couple pounds, in which case he fits what we have pretty well."

"Okay, gentlemen, would you like to visit Mr. Simsek with me?"

William Tell

Chapter Nineteen

3:46 PM
121 East 90th Street

Tommy parked at a fire hydrant down the block from where Harry Simsek lived. They approached the buildings. They saw no Simsek name on any of the bells. However, there was a "Contact the super" sign with a matching phone number and "H. Simsek" on it taped up above the bells and mailboxes in the vestibule of the building.

As the three detectives discussed what to do next, an older woman, about seventy, wearing a long coat and walking with a cane, began to make her way up the stairs.

"Hello, ma'am," Tommy said, revealing the detective shield he had clipped to his belt. We're looking for the super. Do you know where we might find him?"

"Harry? Harry the super, right?" she asked, but before Tommy could answer, she said, "Yes, sir. You gentlemen can find him in the basement. He has the basement apartment down there," pointing around and down the steps they were all standing on to the doorway under the stoop.

"Thank you so much, dear." Tommy replied.

"Don't bother going down there now, though; he's not there."

"Oh no, do you know where he might be?"

"Yes, he's right there, walking down the block right now with the red plaid jacket on."

Tommy cocked his head in disbelief, both at their luck in having the guy they were looking for walk toward them and at how long it took this woman to tell them he was walking down the block rather than the apartment's location.

"Thank you, dear, you've been a big help."

The three detectives stepped off the stoop, and as Harry came close, Miguel and Jimmy stepped to the curb. As Harry got closer, he had no choice but to be surrounded by the three men. As he made it to the iron fence and steps that led to the basement, Harry knew something wasn't right and stepped a bit quicker, trying to pass the detectives by avoiding the entrance to his apartment. Tommy's already high alert status jumped a few points as he did this. He roughly grabbed Harry by his jacket, twisting him off balance and into the fence of the building.

"Police don't move!" he shouted as he forced Harry against the iron, pinning one leg against it with his knee while grabbing Harry's wrist. Jimmy jumped in, grabbing the other. The bag containing a sandwich and a bottle of soda that Harry was carrying hit the floor.

"What, what, what is this?" Harry shouted in defiance.

"Keep your hands where I can see em," Tommy said as he quickly frisked him, removing first a folding knife with a six-inch blade from his jacket pocket, and dropping it onto the sidewalk, then a package of Marlboro cigarettes, some folded up cash in a rubber band, and his wallet, all of which lay on the sidewalk as Miguel picked each item up and placed it on the steps of the stoop.

"What is this?" Harry adamantly demanded.

"We need to have a conversation with you; we have some questions we want answered."

"So, why you roughing me up? You couldn't just ask?"

"My first question, Harry, may answer that. Why were you avoiding your apartment and trying to get past us like you did?"

Harry said nothing for a moment. "Self-preservation," he answered.

"How so?"

"You look in the mirror today? You look like a tough guy, and well, the way you three were standing here, especially the young blood there," Harry said, nodding at Jimmy. It looked like he wanted to give someone a beatdown. Well, yeah, it looked like you were looking for someone, and I didn't want that someone to be me. It seems like it is me though, so what? What did I do? What do you want to know?"

"You're Hamza Simsek, yes?"

"Something tells me you know that already. Yes, everyone calls me Harry, though."

"Okay, Harry, you're going to come to the precinct with us and answer a few questions, okay?"

"The 21st?"

"Yes, the 21st."

"Do I need a lawyer?"

"Are you guilty of anything?"

"I been guilty my whole life, but nothing to warrant this, no."

"Then you don't need a lawyer. Turn around; I gotta cuff you for the ride, okay?"

"Do you gotta cuff me, man? Am I under arrest?"

"Yeah, I need to for our safety."

"If I ain't under arrest, then I don't want the cuffs on."

"Listen, Harry," Miguel interjected. "You see this knife? It's more than four inches; we can arrest you for that. And lookey lookey, you see this little tin foil inside this box of Marlboros?

"Oh, fuck me," He mumbled.

"Yeah, something tells me there's a little white powder in there that we can arrest you for as well, so how about you stop complaining, come downtown with us and let us ask the questions. That work for you?"

"Alright, alright, let's take a ride." Harry begrudgingly conceded.

***

4:40 21st Precinct Detective Interview Room, The Box.

Tommy led Harry into the interview room and had him sit in the chair on the far side. He took his seat opposite Harry on the other side of the small table, and Jimmy sat on the bench that ran along the wall with the two-way mirror in it to the observation room, where Miguel looked on and took notes.

Tommy began, "Alright, Harry. I have a list of questions for you. Please don't jerk me around. You seem like a regular guy, and if everything goes smoothly here, you'll be on your way in no time. However, if you decide to be difficult or lie to me, well then, you may be with us for a while."

Harry stared at Tommy indignantly; he was obviously uncomfortable, and this agitated state raised Tommy's suspicions.

"Yeah, I get it, if I give you a hard time, you're gonna try to fuck up my life," Harry replied, still staring at Tommy.

"Alright then, let me get to know you a little. I know where you live, obviously. What do you do for a living?"

"I'm the super at the building you picked me up at."

"How long you been there?"

"Over nine years."

"What did you do before that?"

"I was a super."

"Where?"

"Different building, decent one over on the west side, West 81ˢᵗ Street."

"How long were you there?"

"Bout ten years."

"This a better gig?"

"Nah, not at all, not by a long shot."

"So why the move?"

"I lost that job, disagreed with a tenant, stupid nonsense over how he put his trash out, guy complained, threw a real fit, and the management company, of course, took the tenant's side, and that was it, ten years down the drain."

"That's a shame, Harry. Don't seem fair after ten years of service?"

"Nope, it ain't fair, not fair at all."

"Are you a sportsman, Harry?"

"I don't play any sports, no, but I do watch sports. I do a little betting on football and basketball. Is that what you're asking?"

"How about fishing or hunting? You into that?"

"Yeah, I do a little hunting. Got a place in the Catskills, little cabin I go up and do a little hunting every season, why?"

"With what? What is your weapon of choice?"

"For a long time, it was a Marlin 30-30, but last couple times I used a Henry 45-70."

"Oooh, big round."

"If you're gonna kill something, you only want to shoot it once."

"You ever use a bow?"

"Yeah, occasionally. That's a bit harder, though; you gotta get closer."

"How about a crossbow?"

"Nah, never, not enough power. You'd have to be right up on top of something to hit it with a crossbow."

Tommy paused momentarily, then continued, "So you've never owned a crossbow?"

"No, never," Harry was becoming more anxious.

"Let me ask you, have you ever been arrested before?

Harry paused and took a breath, and his stare became more pensive as he tried to figure out what Tommy really wanted. "I'm sure you know I have." He said in an increasingly angry yet soft and controlled tone with a highly sinister sound and feel.

"You're right Harry, I do know you have, now back to when we first started this conversation, and we decided you weren't going to bullshit me?"

"What are you talking about? I'm playing it straight with you, Detective."

"Why were you fired from your last job?"

"I told you; it was a tenant…"

Tommy cut him off, "Stop right there. I know why you were fired, Harry. Now tell me why."

Harry's face flushed a bit, and he adjusted himself in his chair, little signs that Tommy was getting to him.

"Okay, okay it was this little bitch, this little fucking bitch from the management office that got me let go."

"There you go, truth ain't so hard now, is it? Tell me the story."

"No big thing, Detective, I asked her out a couple of times, and she reported me to the boss for sexual harassment, complete bullshit, all I did was ask her out, she said no, then a couple weeks later I asked her again, then she had me fired."

"Really?"

"Yeah, that was it."

"I read the complaint, said you called her over twenty times, came to the office at least ten, and on two occasions ran into her in the street near her apartment in Astoria… So, Harry, I gotta think, even if this complaint is half wrong, you were harassing the shit out of this woman?"

"Bullshit, bullshit, that little bitch was a liar, you see, no time, I got no time at all for that arrest!"

"How about the previous arrest? Tell me about that."

"More bitch bullshit."

"Tell us."

"Nothing to it, I met this other miserable bitch in a bar, The P&G over on Broadway, I walk her home we kiss a little on a car, I drop her off at her place next thing I know cops pick me up and arrest me for making out with her, again no time served."

"You're killing me here, Harry. Do you not think I read the reports? Says you forcibly kissed her, reached up under her dress and ripped her panties off before digitally raping her, that's not nothing." Tommy stated flatly, trying to keep his cool.

"It was nothing, it went nowhere, again no time… I got no time, Detective, because they had shit on me, and you know it, and digital rape? What the fuck is digital rape?"

"Means you fingered her against her will, asshole," Jimmy interjected.

"Bullshit, all bitch bullshit!" He replied loudly and angrily.

"Okay, okay, let's forget about the arrests for a moment. You said you never owned a crossbow, correct? That is what you just said a few minutes ago, right?"

"Yes, correct, that is correct," Harry said, his head now spinning in confusion.

"Okay, then. I want you to tell me another story now, and take your time because in this one, I think you're a bit of a hero, a stand-up guy doing the right thing, in my opinion, but I need to get your side of the story, please."

Harry paused for a moment. Tommy could see him loosen up a little physically. "What story is this, Detective?"

"Tell me about the time. It looks like just a couple of years ago, you caught two kids breaking into the basement of one of your buildings on 90th Street."

"Oh yeah, I remember that, these two little nig…" Harry stopped for a moment, "Black kids were breaking into my apartment, not the building's basement, they were trying to get into my fucking apartment and I caught them and held them for you guys to come arrest them, and then…" Harry froze. Something clicked inside his head, and he froze and went silent until Tommy asked,

"What? Then what, Harry, what happened next?"

Harry again began to flush, and he stared into Tommy's eyes with contempt, "I know what you're up to, Detective, I see what you're up to you sneaky motherfucker, well I got one, just one more word for you, Detective, and you know what that word is?"

Tommy lifted his head slightly. "What's that, Harry?"

"Lawyer." Then again louder, "Lawyer motherfucker!"

Tommy said nothing more, and he and Jimmy got up and left the room, locking Harry inside. Then, they joined Miguel in the observation room.

Jimmy immediately began, "So he lawyered up, what are we going to do now?"

"We don't have much on this guy, unfortunately, but there's no way we're letting him go, lawyer or no lawyer. We'll hold him on the knife and drugs, do a deeper investigation on him, see if we can find anything to link him to our victims, we'll get with the district attorney's office, get a warrant to search his apartment and see if anything there links him to the crimes, but…" Tommy paused.

"But what?" both Jimmy and Miguel asked in unison.

"Right now we got nothing on this guy, that's what, nothing more than a few lies, a pocketknife and a small tin of cocaine."

William Tell

Chapter Twenty

Tommy and Jimmy processed Harry for the knife and the small amount of cocaine they found on him, they explained to the team at the district attorney's office that was formed to prosecute the William Tell case, that Hamza Simsek was a suspect, pending further investigation and that they needed to make sure the judge didn't let him walk the next day after his arraignment, and requested a warrant be written up for Harry's residence.

They returned to the precinct at 11:53 PM; by then, the rest of the Task Force had left for the day. They both signed out. As they left the building and began to walk in different directions, Jimmy called to Tommy,

"Hey, Tommy, wait up." Then, he ran the fifteen or so yards to where Tommy stood waiting.

"Hey man, I know it's been a long day, but could I buy you a beer? And, and maybe we could bullshit a little before we head home?"

At that moment, all Tommy could think of was sleep, but he could see Jimmy wanted to talk, so he agreed.

"Sure, Jimmy, let's grab a beer. No real drinking tonight, though. We gotta be back here in the morning, and I'm already beat, so just a couple and no shots, cool?"

"Of course, no shots. I just want to talk a bit, that's all."

Tommy hailed a cab, and they took a short ride to Finnegan's Wake on 73rd Street and 1st Avenue. It was a quiet place, one of Tommy's mother's favorite spots. Tommy thought it would be the perfect place for a quiet beer with Jimmy, and when they arrived, he was proven right. The dining area was empty, and there were only six people at the bar, all engaged in their own conversations.

"What'll it be, fellas?" the thin, rosy-faced barman dressed in a white shirt and black tie of about fifty asked.

"Bottle of Bud," said Tommy, "Coors Light" said Jimmy, as they both took stools halfway down the bar, removing their jackets and hanging them on the back of their stools before they sat.

"So, let's get to it, Jimmy, what you wanna talk to me about?"

"Ahh, well, I guess, well, I guess I just want to ask if you're disappointed about working with me."

Tommy stared at Jimmy for a second in disbelief, "What the fuck you talking about? I love working with you. Where's this nonsense coming from?"

"Well, alright, well, a few weeks ago, before we all got pulled into the serial killer shit, I don't know if you remember, or, or if I'm reading too much into it, but the Lu and I came in at start of tour, and if you remember he announced that I had made the Sergeant's list, and I don't know I got the feeling like you didn't give a shit."

Jimmy took a breath, then continued. "Listen, I don't know how to say this, but I look up to you, Tommy. After my father, you've been my best mentor on this job. I watch and I listen, and I, I really do pay attention and take to heart the lessons you've given me, I don't know, I'm feeling, fuck me I sound like half a fag telling you this, but it's been eating at me that maybe, maybe you don't like working with me?"

Tommy leaned back in his stool and looked at Jimmy for a second or two, a slight grin appearing on his face, "No, no, Jimmy, I very much like working with you. In fact, well, you know what, let me apologize. The other day when the Lu announced you made the sergeants list, if I seemed as though I wasn't happy for you, it wasn't that I didn't care, alright, it was because I really do like working with you and to be honest I think you have everything it takes to be fucking great at this job, okay, you get that? Not a good detective, but a great detective, and so yeah, maybe, maybe I was a little disappointed, and I'm sorry if it showed on my face. But no, no, I'm certainly not disappointed in you, my friend, far from it. I was disappointed that you would be leaving the detective bureau and going back on patrol, which I think will be a loss to this squad and the city. You got that?"

Jimmy sheepishly smiled and looked down at the floor with joy and embarrassment, now knowing he had created a situation in his head that didn't exist.

"Listen, Jim, so few people can really do this job. Really, what is there? Maybe twenty percent of us really kick ass at this job, then another fifty who do what they're supposed to do but no more, and you can't blame them for that, and then that last thirty percent, well we could outright fire them, but then there'd be no one to show up at the parades would there? No, Jimmy, you are good at this job, and I would definitely put you into that top twenty percent, and one day now, you'll be boss of your own squad, then probably a squad commander like Bricks, and I know you're going to be terrific in both those positions, I'm just sorry you won't be a Detective anymore, because good, I mean excellent detectives are few and far between."

"Thanks, Tommy. Thank you very much. I do think we have a good team right now, though, don't you?"

"I love this team, Jimmy. Stein is serious business. He may come off as a curmudgeon, but he is a true detective. Doreen is absolutely Aces. I love everything about her, and unless she goes and takes a Sergeant's test too, I think she could be a great detective. Clay is really one of the hardest-working cops or detectives I have known on this Job, and Bricks is top notch, couldn't ask for a better commander. I am truly blessed to be working with all of you."

"Sergeant Browne? I didn't hear him get mentioned?" Jimmy asked with a slight smirk on his face.

"You know what, Browne is not a bad guy at all. He does his job very well, he could definitely work on his communication skills a bit, and not worry about the politics of the precinct so much, but in the end, I think he's a good and decent man, and I don't mind working for him one bit."

With that, Tommy turned to the bartender and gave him a nod.

"Yes, sir? Another round?" The bartender asked.

"Please, two more beers, and a shot of Jameson for everyone at the bar, including yourself… My friend here made the Sergeant's list, and I couldn't be more proud of him, even if that means I'm losing the fucker."

"I thought you said no shots, Tommy?" Jimmy asked.

"I didn't know this would be a celebration, Jimmy." The bartender passed the shots around, and Tommy made a toast: "Here's to Sergeant Colletti. May his life be long and his troubles be few!"

A unified shout of "To Sergeant Colletti" was heard, followed by the shot glasses hitting the bar one by one.

William Tell

Chapter Twenty-One

The following morning, Tommy and Jimmy looked a little ragged as they dragged themselves into the precinct, but although both were hurting from a few too many beers and shots the night before, it was a mental break and a small bit of relief they both desperately needed.

Tommy received a message from the District Attorney's office, and they managed to have Hamza Sistek held without bail pending further investigation. There is no word on a warrant yet. Although this was good news for the team, it was far from a win, but it did buy them a bit of time.

Tommy put together a package with everything he thought would help Roya do her thing and dig into Simsek.

Miguel was able to find four more images of what he believed to be William Tell from various locations surrounding the Madison O'Neal homicide, all of which were very weak and similar to the first ones he had, one of which was promising. It was in color, and showed enough of his face that they could determine that it was indeed a beard and glasses William Tell was wearing, and that he appeared to be Caucasian, an additional and unusual thing that Miguel discovered was that the bag which Tell had been carrying in all the other images now seemed to be a violin case.

While cross-referencing all his images, Miguel believed a couple more could indeed be violin cases.

"A violin case?" Tommy and Doreen said in unison, followed by "Jinx! You owe me a soda, Mr. Man," From Doreen.

"Victim number four, Madison O'Neal, played the violin?" Tommy stated and asked simultaneously, "Doreen, do us a favor, please, and get a hold of Audra Murphy. I want to question her again, and here." He handed her a $20 bill. "Go get that soda I owe you, and please get me a cold Pepsi. I need some cold fizzy caffeine to clear my head this morning and get anybody anything they want as well."

An hour or so later, Doreen had made arrangements to have Tommy meet Audra in her apartment when she finished her shift at 7:00 PM. And at around that same time, Tommy got a call from Gil,

"Hey, Gil, what's up pal?"

"We got another letter, Tommy, when do…"

"We'll be there in less than an hour, thanks."

1:18 PM
The Herald Building

Tommy, Doreen, Jimmy, and Joe sat around the table in the same office with Gil and Robert Blume again.

"We understand you have made an arrest in this case." Blume asked.

"We've made an arrest related to this case."

"What's that mean exactly, Keane?" Blume said, somewhat agitated.

"Means just that, Bob, we grabbed a guy yesterday, as you obviously know, who we are suspicious of, but to be honest, we got nothing serious on him, and a severe lack of evidence as well at the moment."

"So, is he a suspect, a person of interest?"

"Right now, he's nothing more than a hope and a prayer, to be honest. I don't know, he's being held pending investigation, and if he didn't have a knife and a little bit of blow on him when we grabbed him, he'd be a free man now, that's how little we have. He fits the description, and he has sexually related priors, and is known to have once owned a crossbow, but that's all we got, and we're looking into him right now as we speak."

Tommy then raised his index finger as if to shush Robert Blume, and he read the most recent letter from William Tell.

THAT'S FOUR BITCHES AND
WHORES !!

THERE WILL BE MORE !!!
HOW MANY MORE ??
ARE YOU KEEPING SCORE ??

RIGHT NOW ITS WILLIAM TELL
FOUR
NYPD ZERO !!

I MAY BE THE INCEL KING

BUT I AM NO SIMP !!

BITCHES WILL BE
PUNISHED

REVENGE IS MINE !!

"Does this letter mean the guy you have in custody is innocent?" Gil asked.

"No," Tommy said with a disconcerting sigh. You see the postmark? This was dropped in the mail two days ago. Our guy could have sent it the day before we picked him up."

"Does the postmark help you guys?" Blume asked.

"Unfortunately, no," Joe answered. We have traced every letter sent to each of the various newspapers so far, and they are all being mailed from different neighborhoods. The post office can't tell which boxes they've been dropped in, but this guy is obviously dropping them in various neighborhoods because he doesn't want us tracing them back to him somehow."

As Joe spoke, Tommy placed the paper into an evidence bag and stood up to leave.

"Is that it, Keane? You're just going to take the letter and run? Listen, we had a deal that you would share some info with us if we cooperated with you and kept our reporting as tight and factual as possible, but so far, we are getting our asses kicked by our competitors for some bullshit agreement of fair play, and what do we have, nothing, you're giving us nothing." Blume said aggressively, his broad face began to turn red and his brow began to bead with sweat.

In contrast, Tommy replied calmly, "You're right, Bob, I've given you very little, because I have nothing to give. So far these murders have been extremely clean, almost professional in nature, fast clean executions, of absolutely innocent young women who could not possibly deserve this, I'm at a loss, we got shit, so if you like, print what you want, print ridiculous lies and fabrications, fantastic theories, print whatever you like, it is what you so called journalists love to do anyway, that's how you sell papers and subscriptions right? With wild click baity headlines with no hint of truth, so go ahead, cause you're already good at that, but when it's over, when the smoke is clear, please don't ask me for the inside story, because I'll be too tired and just fed up to share it."

And with that, Tommy left the room, and the rest of the Task Force followed.

***

7:34 PM
Audra Murphy's apartment

Tommy and Doreen made their way up the stairs to find Audra waiting with the door open for them. She was looking a bit haggard. It had been a long few days since the loss of her sister Madison.

"Hey, Audra, thanks for giving us this time. This is my partner, Detective Doyle."

"Hello, Detective Doyle, how ya doing?"

"Very well, thank you. I am so sorry for your loss."

"Thank you, it's been really strange trying to come to terms with it, and I, well, I'm in a fog most of the time, not sleeping, oversleeping, just trying to keep my head on straight, it's been really hard."

"Come have a seat," Tommy said. We have some pictures to show you and some questions to ask."

The three sat around the small oak kitchen table that they had sat at a few days prior. He laid out several stills they had taken from different surveillance cameras around the crime scenes.

"I know these are fairly weak images, Audra, but is there anything you recognize about the man in these photos?"

Audra studied each of them intently, then once she looked at them all, she looked at them again, a tear running down her cheek. She looked at Tommy and said,

"No, I'm so sorry, I don't recognize anything."

She paused momentarily, and before Tommy or Doreen could reply to what she had just said, she continued, "It looks like he's carrying a violin case. Isn't that odd?"

"Yes... We noticed that and thought the same thing, and your sister Madison, she also..." Audra cut Tommy off.

"Played the violin."

Audra sat and looked closer at the photos. She studied them as hard as she could as Tommy and Doreen looked on silently.

"Remember you and the other detective who was here last time asked me, Detective Keane, about any creeps bothering us?"

"Yes, I do," Tommy replied.

"Madison, maybe three or so months ago, had taken two lessons from a guy, violin lessons from a guy who plays viola for some large symphony, supposedly a fantastic musician and impresario who also had a highly popular string trio that plays all over the country. She was excited to take the lessons because he was a lefty, same as Madison, and she had never studied with another lefty."

"Wait?" Tommy interrupted her, "This guy was left-handed?"

"Yeah, just like Madison, and she really liked the idea of learning from such a skilled professional who was also left-handed, just like she was, but she didn't go back to him after the second lesson… I didn't get the whole story, but she said he was odd during their first lesson, and after the second one, he asked her out. When she said no, he got mad and asked her why she wouldn't go out with him. She said he kept asking until she told him he just wasn't her type. She said the guy got teary-eyed after she said that, and then, well then, there was no way she was going to go to another lesson with him."

"Do you remember his name?" He asked almost aggressively as excitement built up inside him, thinking this might be the break that would lead him to William Tell.

"No, not right now. I don't know if I ever knew it, but let's search her room again."

The three spent the better part of an hour looking through everything in Madison's room and the rest of the apartment.

Tommy already had Madison's cell phone in custody as part of the investigation, as with all the victims in the case. So far, nothing of value has been received regarding messages, calls, or location pings that have interested the Task Force. This would have been three months ago. 'No one would have thought to look at messages from three months ago,' he thought. 'Could this be our window? Could this be our man?'

Tommy and Doreen finished with Audra, thanked her for her time, and said they'd be in touch. Then, they headed back to the precinct. As Tommy drove, Doreen called Jimmy, Joe, and Therese, who had just signed out, to tell them about the development of the left-handed viola player. With that call placed, they returned to the office, and all five dug into this latest information.

The Task Force office buzzed as everyone typed away on their computers, searching for anything that might lead them to a left-handed viola player.

As everyone searched every possible angle, Tommy ran downstairs to the property room, retrieved each of the victims' cell phones, and called Roya.

"Hey, Tommy, what's up?"

"Can we meet?"

"When?"

"Now, it's important."

"I, well yeah, of course, I'm downtown, out with a friend, but I can make it uptown if it's important."

"Very important. Listen, catch a cab to 67th and 3rd, text me when you're about halfway up, and I'll come meet you."

"Will do!"

Roya texted Tommy about fifteen minutes later, and he walked over to 3rd Avenue and waited for her to arrive. She exited the taxi, and Tommy approached her, handing her a plastic shopping bag with the four phones. Without greeting her, he immediately began.

"These are our four victims' cell phones, the one in the bag marked Madison O'Neal, we think had calls or texts from William Tell about three or four months ago. I don't have time to fuck around and get into them properly through the right channels, if this is our guy we need to know now, they should be talking about violin or viola lessons, and again approximately three maybe four months ago."

"Got it," Roya replied.

"Listen, I'm not done. Check the others for the same number and cross-reference them however you can. I don't know what you do or how you do it, but please do what you can to find out who this guy may be!"

"Got it, Tommy. I'll be all over this tonight."

"Thank you, Roya. Your help means the world to me." He kissed her on the forehead and hailed a cab, which took her home.

When he returned to the precinct, it was almost midnight. Doreen had a list of every symphony orchestra active in the New York City area, as well as every string trio she could find. At that late hour, no one seemed to be answering phones in any of the Symphony headquarters. Still, she did send an inquiry to each via email, she also had Jimmy reach out to every string trio she had listed via email or Facebook, looking for information, but as of yet, they hadn't received a single reply.

Joe was searching through the NYPD database for any links to homicides relating to music, musicians, violins, violas, left-handed, absolutely anything he could think of to catch a break and shed light on who could fit in with this new information they had just come across.

At 2:00 AM, Tommy called it quits. "Listen, we've all been breaking our ass here for the last sixteen hours, let's all get some rest so we're not complete shit come tomorrow. I'll message everyone so we have the full team come tomorrow, well check every symphony, music school, music store, we will search everything we can and fuck me we will figure out who this Willaim Tell is! But we're all going to need some rest first."

William Tell

Chapter Twenty-Two

Day 21
8:30 AM

Tommy was awoken again by the Fantastic Plastics playing Troublemaker on his phone. Lying on his stomach, he reached over with his right hand and turned it off. Then, he felt JoJo pawing at him, anxious to meet the morning and go for his first walk of the day.

Tommy sat up in the complete darkness of his room and checked his phone, hoping he had slept through a message from Roya saying she had cracked the case, but there was nothing.

So, he stood up, pulled on a pair of sweatpants and a hoodie, then his car coat, and stuffed his .38 Centennial Revolver into the jacket pocket. He took little JoJo for a walk in the crisp, cool March air.

When he returned home, he said hello to his mother, who, as usual, was pouring coffee as she puffed away on a cigarette. He then showered, brushed his teeth, and dressed for the day. He glanced at his phone every few minutes, hoping for a call or message from Roya, but none arrived.

Tommy arrived at the precinct at 9:54 AM to find Therese, Miguel, and Gloria already in and typing away. Everyone else began to file in one by one, Jimmy with a large box of Dunkin' Donuts and a gallon of coffee.

Tommy quickly briefed the entire team again on what they had learned the evening before from Audra Murphy. The information Tommy and Doreen had gleaned was scant, but he believed it would be the key to unlocking these murders: the violin cases seen in the surveillance video, a left-handed viola player, and the fact that the handwriting expert said whoever wrote the letters was most likely left-handed were simply too odd to be coincidence. He knew they now had something to go on.

"Jimmy, do us a favor and find out if Harry Simsek plays viola. Also, what happened to the warrant to search his apartment?"

At this point, Tommy was seriously doubting Harry Simsek was their man. Of course, his doubts meant nothing compared to facts, but Harry, as creepy as he was, as much as he fit the description on paper, just didn't ring true to him, but he knew he had to follow up.

11:29 AM

Tommy and the rest of the team sat in their makeshift office in the 2-1, each looking over different aspects of their joint investigation, the paperwork, photographs, and different sites on the computer, searching for anything they may have missed that might just be the clue or the break they needed to lead them to this left-handed viola player and William Tell.

Doreen picked up the ringing landline on her desk. "Oh, for Christ's sake," she said loudly, "We have another victim," speaking loud enough for the entire team to hear, "306 West 75th Street."

Tommy stood up without saying a word, grabbed his coat from the back of his chair, and headed toward the door. The other five members on duty followed him out of the building to their cars and then drove to the scene.

12:12 PM

Tommy and the team pulled up in front of the red brick building, where two uniformed officers from the 20th precinct stood out in front, talking. As Tommy and Doreen led the rest of the team towards the door, one of the officers said, "2nd floor Detectives," as he opened and held the door for all five detectives as they entered.

On the second floor, they found two more uniformed officers, their sergeant, and three detectives from the 2-0 Squad.

"Hey, Tommy, how you doing? It's been a minute, hasn't it?" asked Tommy's old friend, Johnny Letterio, with whom he had worked in Bronx Narcotics some ten years prior.

"Oh, Johnny, how you doing pal? And yeah, I haven't seen you in forever. How you been?" Tommy replied. Both men shook hands and embraced, each delivering a hardy double slap onto the other's back.

"Never better. I heard about your shooting, I mean, who hasn't, right? … How you feeling?"

"Other than this fucking murderer terrorizing the city, I'm about a hundred percent, and really I can't complain."

"You never were one to complain anyway… So, this is what we got for you, Tom: one Angela DelVecchio, twenty-eight years of age, lives here with a roommate. That's who found her, a young lady named Andrea Postella- a likable girl, very shaken up at the moment, for obvious reasons." Johnny continued,

"Miss Postella came home maybe an hour ago, finds the door closed but unlocked, opens it up, calls out for Angela, walks in, and boom, sees this in the dining area here. She immediately runs out of the apartment, dropping these bags on the floor, and calls 911, and well, here we are."

"Where's Andrea now?" Tommy asked.

"She's in a car downstairs having a soda with Detective Mostecelli, from our team… So, you see, our girl Miss DelVecchio took an arrow to the front left neck, slash, shoulder area, right? Then a second arrow here, to her right temple, now without touching nothing, I think our Miss DelVecchio put up a fight."

Tommy interjected, "Looking at what I'm looking at here, I think you're right, Johnny, but please continue. I want to hear your thoughts and find out where you're going with this."

At this point, Tommy squatted next to the body, and Doreen and Joe stood behind Johnny with their hands in their pockets. As Johnny continued, they all took in the scene of the body and its surroundings. Jimmy and Therese were still in the hallway, taking the names and shield numbers of everyone on the scene.

"Alright, well, before we look at her, I see this stuff on the table is all knocked over and a mess. I also see that stuff about three to four feet away on the countertop is also knocked over and a bit of a jumble, but otherwise, this place is as clean as a fat kid's tray after lunch period. I mean, take a look, the place is immaculate."

Johnny took a breath.

"Now look at our Miss DelVecchio, beautiful young lady, all put together nice, but her shirt is half untucked, her hair is more disheveled than I would expect from just crashing onto the floor after taking the arrow to the shoulder, which I'm gonna guess, wouldn't have knocked her on her ass anyway. And then look at her, she's got an arrow in the left shoulder, pointing out one way, and the other arrow in the right temple, pointing out the other way, so I think our shooter gets in here, however he gets in here, and hits her on the left side first. But Miss DelVecchio ain't having it, so they get into a bit of a tussle, all this stuff is knocked down, our shooter overcomes her and knocks her to the floor and is somehow able to get a second arrow off, but this time hitting her on the right side of the head probably killing her dead directly there…"

Johnny paused again.

"Look, look how she is contorted here between the table and the countertop, and how the arrows are coming in from opposite sides, it just don't look right. Also, her left hand middle finger has a broken nail, and I will bet you anything, once Crime Scene is done in here, and we move the body and can do a thorough search, we find that nail here in this room, and if we're lucky our Miss DelVecchio will have a little skin and DNA under her nails for us, so when we finally collar this fucker, we'll have him cold."

Tommy took it all in, everything Johnny said about the scene, and Angela DelVechio's crumpled little body.

"I think you're spot on Johnny… and man I hope you're right about some DNA; we desperately need something to tighten the noose on this fucker."

Tommy stood up and looked at Johnny and the rest of his team, taking his eyes off Angela's body.

"Alright, let's all get out of here until Crime Scene shows up for their bit, everyone is notified, yes?"

"Yeah, everyone has been notified and is on their way, Tom," Letterio answered.

***

Within an hour, both Crime Scene and Angela Marcus from the Medical Examiner's Office arrived. Crime Scene took their time and scoured the apartment and the rest of the interior of the building for evidence, anywhere they believed they might find something. In this case, some small bits of interesting evidence were recovered.

Three small smears of blood were detected near the kitchen, two more on the staircase, and one inside the building's entrance door.

Several relatively short, coarse brown hairs were found in the apartment; at first glance, they were believed to be from a man's beard.

There were mountains of samples of hair, both long and short, and dozens of clothing fibers recovered from the apartment, hallways, stairways, and entranceway of the building. Still, these particular hairs and the relatively small blood smears brought tremendous hope to the team.

Once Crime Scene had finished, Angela Marcus began her examination as Tommy and the rest of the team looked on. The cause of death was apparent, and Marcus didn't even bother to state it.

After her cursory inspection of the top side of Angela DelVecchio, Marcus, along with Tommy, turned her over so Marcus could examine the remainder of Miss DelVecchio's body, and in doing so, revealed the broken fingernail on the floor beneath her, as well as a dented can of Progresso Clam Chowder.

Angela Marcus continued to poke and prod the young woman's corpse in an attempt to ascertain any clues, then looked to Tommy, who was squatting next to her, and then over to the rest of the team, who were all standing by with notable interest, and began to speak.

"Okay, so let's start here, you see there is a slight mark right here at her hairline, and when I touch her here it feels slightly raised, I am going to assume our victim was struck with something hard, and my guess is that it may be this can of chowder we found under her body here… Now, look at this…" She continued raising the hand with the broken nail, holding out Delvechio's index finger, "I can see here, what I believe will prove to be skin and a little bit of blood from our assailant, and I'm going to assume the person we're looking for is going to have some serious scratches, because the force she used yanked this nylon wrap right off of her finger," She said holding the detached fingernail up between her thumb and forefinger.

ME. Marcus then stood up and stared down at Angela DelVecchio's body as she removed her latex gloves. "This one's not a blonde." She said flatly, "I imagine the theory of this animal only attacking blondes is broken now."

"Looks that way," Tommy replied softly and somberly.

"I should be doing her autopsy around two tomorrow. You can come by around then or call me, and I'll tell you where we are. Good luck, Keane, and try to get some sleep; you're not looking yourself."

***

Once ME Marcus was done, Tommy and the team did a thorough search of the body before having it removed. They then searched every inch of the apartment. This search came up with nothing more than what they had before they started.

Still, that little bit they did have was a lot; they knew they would now receive DNA from skin under the fingernails and possibly the hair and blood samples. This murder, as awful as it was, would provide the evidence needed to secure a conviction when they finally caught up with William Tell.

Tommy brought Angela DelVechio's roommate, Andrea Postello, back to the precinct for her interview. Andrea was too shaken up to return to the apartment and, unfortunately, had nothing of interest or value to add to the investigation during her interview. She asked if she could wait in the squad room as she would have her father drive down from Port Chester, New York, and bring her home rather than stay in the apartment.

Meanwhile, as the search of Angela's apartment and Andrea's interview took place, up on 88th Street, Roya had a breakthrough.

The hours of searches she had put in, combing through everything she could dig up on each of the victims, on the weapon used, on serial and spree killers, seemed to finally pay off with a simple click of a key related to the violin. There was a name; she followed it; Roya began typing feverously, checking and cross-referencing every bit of information that popped up related to it.

4:11 PM

Tommy's phone buzzed. Seeing it was Roya, he stepped into the hallway outside the Squad Room for some privacy.

"Roya, tell me you found something?"

"Milo Belinski is who you're looking for, Tommy. He is twenty-eight years old, and it looks like he was giving Madison violin lessons a little more than three months ago. He's from Ridgefield, Connecticut. I have two possible addresses for him here in the city, one on East 80th and the other on 91st. He appears to be pretty successful with his music; he's played with the Brooklyn Symphony and travels all around with his own trio. I have social media posts of him and his trio playing at Steps Dance Studio on Broadway. I have a ton of stuff to share with you, but it looks like Milo Belinski is who you are looking for."

Tommy was speechless for a second. He took a couple of breaths and stared at the hallway floor until Roya asked, "Tommy, are you there? Did you hear everything I said?"

"Yeah, yes I did, Roya, this is great, thanks," He replied in a somewhat subdued manner, still trying to grasp the fact that Roya may have just handed him his killer. "Listen," he continued, "Text me the correct spelling of his name and his addresses. I'm in the middle of something, but I will contact you shortly to follow up… And thank you so much, Roya, thank you so so much, kid."

Tommy quickly rushed up to the Task Force office. "Listen up! We have a line on our man; his name is Milo Belinski, and he was giving violin lessons to Madison O'Neal. His string trio also played shows at Steps dance studio, so let's get on the phones. We have a couple of warrants to get written, and we need them now!

Chapter Twenty-Three

Tommy called the District Attorney's office and had them begin writing up the two search warrants for Milo's possible apartments, warrants that, under normal circumstances, with so little evidence or proof of residence, would never be approved. But with the severity of this case, and the constant public and media pressure revolving around it, Tommy believed no judge would take the chance politically of not signing them, especially hours after the murder of Angela Delvechio, and then leave Belinski to strike again. Tommy was right; within two hours, he had a warrant for each of Bellinski's possible addresses.

At 6:14, Tommy's phone began to buzz. He didn't recognize the number and answered, "Keane."

"Hi, Detective Keane," It was Audra Murphy. "I found out from a friend that the guy my sister was taking lessons from is named Milo Belinski. I hope this helps."

"Thank you, Audra, and yes, yes dear, that definitely helps. I'll follow up and be in touch soon, okay? Have a good night, dear."

Tommy knew he was on the right track after speaking with Roya, but this sealed the deal, and he made arrangements with the Emergency Service Unit to execute two simultaneous warrants at each of the locations Roya had given him.

***

9:35 PM

Tommy, Doreen, and Miguel stood outside 298 East 80th Street as Emergency Services entered the building and the second-floor apartment, where they believed Milo Belinski stayed.

Meanwhile, at 9:38 PM, Joe, Therese, and Jimmy waited outside 187 East 91st Street as Emergency Services entered the 4th-floor apartment where they also believed Milo Belinski stayed.

ESU secured both locations. A thirty-two-year-old man, Aaron Millings, was detained at the 91st Street location. He claimed that Milo was indeed his roommate, but that was over a year ago, and he no longer lived there, and said they were no longer in touch. However, during the search, he cooperated completely and was taken to the precinct to be interviewed.

The 80th Street location was empty, but it was immediately apparent that Milo Belinski lived there. After beginning the search, it appeared he lived alone, as all the mail was addressed to him, all of the clothing and other belongings appeared to belong to only one individual, and there was only one toothbrush in the bathroom.

It was a small apartment; it wasn't particularly tidy, but it wasn't a mess either. The litter box gave off the odor of cat, one of which Doreen found hiding under the bed in the bedroom, next to three viola cases. She called out to Tommy and Miguel,

"Guys, come see what I have here."

Then, sitting on the hardwood floor, with Tommy and Miguel standing behind her, she opened the first case; inside was a beautiful, shiny viola. She paused for a moment and opened the second case, and again found another viola. The third case was a little older and scuffed up. As she opened it, she let out a slight gasp. There it was, what they all were hoping for, the murder weapon: the crossbow, and with it were two black bolts with red flights.

For the next hour, the team searched through the apartment and collected anything they thought might help their case or help them find Milo Belinski. After completing their search, they employed the help of the 2-1 precinct's plain-clothed Anti-Crime team to sit outside the building if Milo was to return. They then all returned to the office.

Tommy did his best to keep cool and keep his head from spinning. They now knew who their man was after a three-week five-body killing spree; they had the murder weapon and other evidence that would prove forensically crucial, but the killer was still at large.

Doreen and the others had quickly built complete profiles through social media and the computer, including photos and almost everything Milo Belinski had done in the last ten years, but they had no Milo. 'Was he on the lam after the

murder of Angela Delvechio? Did he make a run for
it?' Tommy thought.

"Jimmy, please get with all the hospitals. Let's see if our
Milo had to be seen after his fight with the Delvechio
girl." Tommy asked, "Therese, let's get with the Ridgefield,
Connecticut, Police. See if they have any info on our guy they
can share."

Tommy pulled out his phone. Stepping out of the
office and back into the hallway, he called Roya again:

"Hey, Roya, can you please give me his phone number?
Then hop in a cab, and we'll meet on 67th again. Bring
everything you got for me on this Milo guy."

"Will do, Tommy. I'll message you when I get in the
cab."

As he put his cell back in his pocket, Doreen shouted
from inside the office, "Tommy!"

"What's up?" He asked.

"His trio band thing is playing tonight at Bargemusic;
it's a floating concert hall in Brooklyn right under the Brooklyn
Bridge. Looks like the show goes from 8 -11:30; we gotta move
if we wanna catch him there."

And move they did. Tommy, Doreen, and Therese in
one car and Jimmy, Joe, and Miguel in the other flew down
FDR Drive towards and over the Brooklyn Bridge into
Brooklyn, then made their way to Water Street and the floating
venue. On the drive over, Tommy texted Roya to hold off on
going to 67th as they were on the way to Brooklyn and,
hopefully, Milo Belinski.

As they arrived and exited their vehicles, they could see the place was emptying out as both concert goers and musicians dispersed from the scene and the area into the Brooklyn night.

Frantically, the team set up a perimeter around the exit to observe everyone leaving in an attempt to locate Bilinski. Tommy and Doreen made their way through the crowd and onto the barge, hoping to find him still inside and packing up, but Milo Belinski was not seen on or outside.

Doreen approached a couple of musicians still loading up and chatting on the barge and asked if they knew or had seen Milo. A short, round bass player in his thirties with a beard wearing a tuxedo said, "Yeah, I know that creep," with a bit of disdain.

"Really? Can you tell me where he is? he did play here tonight, didn't he?" Doreen asked excitedly.

"Sorry, Miss, you missed him; he packed up and headed out." The bass player answered as he closed the case on his instrument and snapped it shut.

"Any idea where he may have been going? Is there an after party or something?"

"No, sorry. Our group is heading out for a few beers, but no, he certainly wouldn't be joining us. No one hangs with Milo, not even the guys in his own trio."

"You don't say? Can you tell me why?"

"Listen Miss, I don't want to shit on the guy, is he a friend of yours or something?"

"No, I was looking to take lessons from him." She said, not wanting to ID herself.

"Ahh, I see, well, all I can say is he is one of the best musicians you'll ever meet, but one of the most arrogant, aloof, self-centered bastards as well, if he wasn't so talented, he would have nothing, and I mean nothing to offer the world."

"So, you're not a fan I see," Doreen replied with a friendly smile, trying to encourage him to continue.

"No, he rubs me, well he rubs everyone the wrong way, absolutely amazing musician, he's just not much of a human being," He then leaned in slightly and lowered his voice, "In fact, maybe you should find someone else to take lessons from, he's got a bit of a reputation for being kind of, well, off putting to women, more than once I've heard women I know call him outright scary."

"Really?"

"Yes, really, save your money and find someone else. He's a very strange man; I'm just being honest."

***

11:59 PM 298 East 80th

As Tommy and the rest of the team made their way off the Brooklyn Bridge and onto the FDR Drive, Tony Ramirez and Richie Crowe had been sitting in their beat-up navy blue Rent-a-Wreck Ford Taurus about two car lengths up from the entrance to Milo Belinski's building for a little more than two hours.

Tony and Richie were two of the 2-1's Anti-Crime team, thick-necked, hard-charging go-getters. Both were twenty-eight years of age and two of the most active police officers in the 2-1.

That evening, they sat and waited to see if Belinski would show. Sitting for hours like they did could be highly uncomfortable and mind-numbing. Still, patience was part of the job, and these two were two of the best in the precinct. They sat and listened to the radio, read the paper, did the crossword, and waited, something that was a talent in itself, a talent that on this particular night would pay off.

"Oh, Richie!" Tony said, slapping Richie in the chest with the back of his hand. "Look, here he is. This is our boy. The little guy with a violin case that just came around the corner."

"Fuckin' aye!" Richie replied, and both men casually exited the blue Taurus and made their way towards the entrance of Milo's doorway, never making eye contact with him as they casually had a fake chat.

Milo noticed the officers as they approached, and when they were about eight feet away, he stopped and paused for a second. He didn't make them as police officers, but they did make him nervous. There was something not right, and he could sense it.

Was he about to get mugged or jumped by these two tough guys dressed in blue jeans and sneakers, one in an O.D. green army jacket, the other in a denim jacket over a hoodie, and he still in his tuxedo from the show? He didn't know why he felt what he felt, but it caused him to pause.

That pause was all Tony Ramirez needed to leap into action. He rushed forward, grabbed Milo by his overcoat, and, without warning, threw him onto the sidewalk in less than two seconds.

"Don't hurt me, don't hurt me! My money is in my front pocket. Go ahead and take it, please. I won't fight back; take it."

Tony and Richie laughed, as Richie stood on one of Milo's wrists and Tony roughly forced his other wrist behind his back and cuffed it, then leaning down towards his ear, pressing his knee deep into his back, Tony said softly,

"We got you Milo, you filthy motherfucker, we got you."

Milo then knew what had just happened, and in the next few seconds, as the realization set in, he let out a deep breath. It was a relaxing breath, as if he was relieved that it was the police and not a mugging, also as though he was relieved that his reign of terror had ended.

Tony stood up, and as he did, Richie reached over and gave Tony a high five. Then keyed the mic on his radio: "2-1 Squad, you on the air? 2-1 Squad, can you hear me?"

"10-4 2-1 Squad on the air," Jimmy replied.

"2-1 Crime here. I'm requesting an 85 at 298 East 80th, please. We have a little package for you."

"10-4 2-1 Crime, en route, and less than ten out."

"Very good. 2-1 Squad, no rush; all is well."

In less than ten minutes, both cars pulled up to the scene, and the entire team stepped out. They saw officers Ramirez and Crowe leaning against the wall of 298, casually smoking cigarettes, while Milo Belinski still lay face down on the sidewalk, his viola case by his side just in front of them.

As Tommy and the others approached, Tony pushed himself off the wall and extended his hand toward Tommy, "I think this is who you're looking for, Detective."

Tommy shook Tony's hand and slapped him on the shoulder, then shook Richie's hand, "Looks like you guys did good tonight, thank you both very much, has he…"

Tony cut him off, "Not a word. We haven't asked him a thing, and he hasn't said anything other than telling me where his money was… He thought we were robbing him when we grabbed him, but no, he hasn't said a word, and neither have we. We haven't told him he was under arrest either. I, well, all the work you put into this, I figured you'd like to tell him yourself."

Tommy nodded and smiled a slight smile. He really didn't care who told him he was under arrest, but he appreciated Tony and Richie's gesture, especially in this case.

Tommy leaned over at the waist and looked into Milo Belinski's eyes. "Milo Belinski?"

"Yes," Milo responded almost eagerly.

"You are under arrest for the murders of Heather Mills, Kaylee Reese, Jenna Morrison, Madison O'Neal, and Angela DelVecchio."

William Tell

Milo strained his eyes and neck to look back at Tommy, lifting his head off the sidewalk as much as possible. With a slight smirk and a bit of spittle running out of his mouth, he replied, "Took you long enough."

Chapter Twenty-Four

The team arrived back in the precinct, and as they did, the few officers on duty who were in the house at the time all stopped doing what they were doing to take notice of the serial killer who had been terrorizing the city for the last three weeks.

Tommy was happy the news hadn't reached the media yet, and there were no reporters or news vans outside when they arrived. What a photo op it would have been though. Six detectives, all taller than the perpetrator, who stood five feet five inches, perfectly groomed and wearing a tuxedo, a Brooks Brothers overcoat, and patent leather shoes.

Together, the seven made their way up to the second floor and into the Squad room. Tommy and Jimmy searched Milo and placed him in the cage before notifying the District Attorney's office, and not forgetting to send his friends Gil and Roya a quick text letting them know they had their man.

It took a moment for the room to settle, as the team took over the squad room since the task force office was so small and there was no cell or interview room. Just as everything seemed to get into working order to process the case, Milo, who had remained relatively silent for the past sixty minutes or so since his arrest, other than answering direct questions, spoke out.

He stood at the cell door, almost at attention. Although his clothing had been removed during his search, he was again dressed and all buttoned up in his tuxedo. He looked at Tommy, but when he began to speak, he was addressing the room, which at this point contained all six task force detectives, Brenda, and Lieutenant Bricks.

"Detective Keane," he said loudly and clearly, still looking at Tommy, "It took you and your team a while to catch me, but you did. Kudos to you, sir. I knew you would eventually, and I have been looking forward to meeting you."

Milo paused for a moment.

"I, of course, followed this case intently, online, on television, and in the papers. I was a bit obsessed with it, as you might imagine…" he said with a sickening grin, his eyes blinking with a nervous tic.

"And I was thrilled to know that the much-admired Detective Thomas Francis Keane was the man who was after me. You, sir, have been written about extensively and have quite a reputation online and in the papers. I am surprised you are still a third-grade detective. I can only imagine it is due to your aggressiveness and unorthodox methods." – "Is that the case, Lieutenant Bricks? Is Detective Keane a little too unmanageable for you?"

Lieutenant Bricks said nothing, just stared with disdain as Milo continued his monologue, his blinking slowing but still persistent.

"Well, if he is, tonight is a night to be happy with him. I know it has been three-plus weeks of terror, but I was in a hurry and moving as fast as I could. You see, I knew you would catch me eventually, so I had to try to complete my list as quickly as possible. You know this could have dragged on for months, possibly even years, so I think you all deserve a round of applause for wrapping this case up so swiftly …"

He said as he slowly clapped his hands.

"So, my distinguished task force, tonight you have finally nabbed your man, and it appears to be only three weeks and one day since my reign of terror began… As far as you know anyway."

He finished the sentence smugly, as if he knew something no one else in the room knew.

"And in the spirit of friendship and professional courtesy, I have planned on making our time together as easy as possible. So please, now is the time to take notes, if you must, because as I said, I do intend to make our time together as easy as possible for you noble crime fighters, and confess fully to the crimes I have committed, and to do so in full detail answering every question you may have. Still, I have conditions, and each must be followed to secure my cooperation.

Milo paused again, both for effect and to be polite and wait for someone else to speak.

"What are these conditions?" Lieutenant Bricks asked.

Milo waited a second before answering, again for effect. It was obvious he was a showman, treating his cell as a stage and the task force before him as his audience.

"Well, Lieutenant, Detectives, my requests are straightforward," Milo again paused for a moment, "What I have done will make us all famous. There will be books written about us all, news specials, Netflix documentaries, and for years to come, people will talk about the William Tell killer. That name will be every bit as infamous as Berkowitz, Bundy or Dahmer, so I believe it is important to do everything properly, and to do everything properly, right from the beginning, I will request that you get a reporter, and a real camera up here, not the lousy ones you use in your interrogation rooms to record my confession."

Milo took a deep breath, "I will ask, please, for a pillow and a blanket for this cell, and that you allow me to sleep tonight, and tomorrow we'll have some breakfast and set up for the interview and confession. I will request that a court-appointed lawyer be present, but have no worries; I do intend to cooperate fully. I want my story to be told, and I don't want future authors or media to say I had no legal representation, so, ladies and gentlemen of the William Tell Task Force, will you grant me my requests?"

The room hung silently for a moment. Tommy began to speak, but Lieutenant Bricks cut him off.

"We, here in this office, do not have the final authority to grant you all of your conditions, Mr. Belinski, but what we can do is make an honest effort. We can supply you with a blanket and a pillow, while we discuss the rest with the District Attorney's office and see what they will allow."

"That, Lieutenant Bricks, is a truthful and thoughtful answer, the kind I would expect from a professional like yourself. Thank you, sir, for your honesty. If you will, please contact the district attorney handling my case, and let's get this moving as quickly and easily as possible."

"They have been notified and are on their way… Jimmy, please get Mr. Belinski a pillow and a blanket from the dorm, would you?"

***

Jimmy handed Milo the pillow and blanket through the cell bars. Then, the team and Lieutenant Bricks stepped across the hall to the muster room, leaving Brenda behind to keep an eye on the prisoner. They discussed the odd moment they shared and where they thought they would be taking the rest of the investigation.

Tommy, who's case this was began, "This is a strange fucking development."

Jimmy interjected, "Are you thinking of meeting these assholes demands after all we've been through, Tommy?"

"Yes, I think it's the prudent thing to do. We give him as much as possible to get as much out of him as possible. I mean, honestly, I think we got him cold. Once the DNA comes back from the DelVecchio murder, he'll be toast, but what I don't want, what we can't afford, is any bullshit where the jury only convicts two or three out of the five victims; we want to nail him on every one. So yes, yes, I say we provide him everything we possibly can. Suppose something goes sideways in the days or weeks to come. In that case, we will at the very least have his confessions for each of these girls, which he seems more than willing to give, so even if we have to coddle this fucker, even compliment him on a job well done, I say we play his game until we have every detail down on paper, and film, do we all agree?"

"I agree completely!" A small but loud voice came from the doorway of the muster room, from ADA Jessica Lokietz and her colleague, ADA Jeffery Springer.

"Jessica! Perfect timing. Please come on in, so you heard what I had to say?"

"Yes, we did, and I absolutely agree with you, Detective. Let's give him anything he wants, we'll need to get authorization from my office, but if we can secure some airtight confessions for each of these homicides, I am all for placating to this psychopaths' whims, after all he will be spending the rest of his life in prison, won't he?"

Chapter Twenty-Five

Because of the hour, it took several phone calls and a bit of doing to get themselves ready for the day, but as per Milo Bilinski's request, a public defender, a cameraman, and a reporter were all arranged to be present for his confessions. As Tommy requested, Gil Nunez was arranged to be the reporter present that day.

Milo received a mushroom and Swiss cheese omelet with tomatoes, home fries, coffee, and orange juice from Niels Coffee Shop around the corner. The muster room was reorganized to be used as the staging area for the confessions, as the interview room was too small to accommodate Milo, his public defender, two detectives, two ADAs, a reporter, and a cameraman.

It was a very unusual scene for all involved, more resembling a movie set than any interview any of the professionals involved had ever witnessed.

Milo and his attorney, Martin Rivnek, sat at a corner table with two walls behind them. On the opposite side sat Tommy, Joe, ADA Jessica Lokietz, and, just behind her, her partner Jeffrey Springer. Several feet back and to the side nearest the entrance, the rest of the detectives from the task force, along with Lieutenant Bricks and Gil Nunez, were all seated.

All was placed in position and agreed upon by Milo, with the district attorney's office's permission. After a brief conversation with his court-appointed attorney, Martin Rivnek, Milo said he was under no circumstances to interrupt his confession and that he was indeed there not as a defender but as a witness.

11:42 AM

Everyone was identified for the camera, and the interview and confessions began.

ADA Jessica Lokietz speaking; "Mr. Bilinski, you have admitted to detectives arresting you for the William Tell murders that you are indeed the perpetrator of these killings, and that you are responsible for the deaths of Heather Mills, Kaylee Reese, Jenna Morrison, Madison O'Neal, and Angela DelVecchio. Is that correct, sir?"

Milo leaned in slightly, paused as always for effect, and replied, "Yes, it was me, I, Milo Bilinski, killed each of those women, with malice, intent, and great prejudice."

Although his words were few, they were strong and confident, and it left most in the room, even the detectives who had seen it all, a bit shocked.

Jessica continued, "Mr. Bilinski, I would like to ask you about each of your victims, please."

"Of course, that's why we are here, isn't it... Jessica?"

Milo called Jessica by her first name for the first time and did so with a disgusting familiarity that agitated everyone in the room, which was his intent. Although it garnered no reaction, Milo felt he had hit his mark with this hint of disrespect.

Jessica continued, showing no recognition of his barb, "Please, sir, tell us why you targeted and killed Heather Mills."

"I will, but first, bear with me for a moment. I want to tell you a little bit about myself. You already know much of this, but I want it to be part of the confession and what is being filmed."

He paused, and with no one objecting, continued, his eyes blinking a bit and slightly smiling.

"I was born and raised in Ridgefield, Connecticut, to two decent, loving parents, both of superior intellect. I myself have an IQ of 142. I was a natural musician and excelled with the violin and viola. High School and University were a joke to me; I graduated both a year early, and during these years, my love and admiration for the opposite sex was slowly driven into contempt."

Milo paused for a breath, then continued.

"You see, being brilliant and talented simply wasn't enough for women, at least not the women I was attracted to and believed I should be surrounded by. It seems my height of five feet five and a quarter inches, and my slight lisp, which my grandfather called a hair lip, was also a disqualifier. You see, Jessica, young, attractive women like yourself don't care for talent, do they? No, not today. Today, it is all physical attraction and, of course, money, but I could never pay for it. Believe it or not, Jessica, I wanted love, I hoped for companionship."

Milo paused again to let that last line sink in.

"So let me answer your question, Jessica. Heather … Heather Mills. I first encountered her at Steps dance school on Broadway. On two occasions, I had done some live music with my trio there, for different showcases they put on, and when we met, oh my god, what a beauty I thought, but I knew she would never be interested in me. Still, it was she who approached me. She thanked us for the music and said my playing was sublime; she also asked where I was doing other shows she could attend. We had a short but lovely conversation. We met maybe four more times; she was always outgoing and pleasant, and after one of her showcases, I asked her if I could take her for coffee, or to dinner and a movie, and well, that was pretty much it for Heather."

He paused again, and Jessica asked,

"Please explain."

"Well, Heather laughed at me. She outright laughed at me and her exact words were, 'You can't be serious.' I was, and sadly, she thought the idea was preposterous. So, I stalked her for a couple of weeks, waited for her to arrive home one day, and shot her with my crossbow, made sure she did indeed pass from the injury, then left the scene."

He again paused, this time taking a sip of water.

"And that was it for Heather Mills. I crossed her off my list. Shall we continue to Kaylee Reese?"

"If you would like to, yes," Jessica replied.

"Very good. Kaylee Reese was an event planner for a high-end clothing company. She contacted me again through my trio to play a few of her events, and yes, she was another gorgeous woman, wasn't she? So, this was an amazingly similar story to Heather's. We performed at four separate events for Kaylee; I think it was on the third that we had a rather pleasant conversation. I asked her out for a date, and she politely said no. Then, after our fourth show for her and her company, we had a lovely conversation again. I again asked her out for a date, and she again said no; however, this time, she said, 'No, absolutely not. I have no interest in ever dating you; never ask me again.' Or something to that effect, but in an insulting and demeaning tone, so she was added to the list, and about eight weeks later, she was crossed off as she left the pool where she would swim at the neighborhood association on 90th Street with one shot from my crossbow."

"And Jenna Morrison?" Jessica Asked.

"Jenna rented me my apartment, she was also lovely, and so full of personality. Oh my, I think it would be hard for anyone not to like Jenna. She had shown me several apartments before we settled on the one I live in now, where the detectives picked me up last night, rather roughly, I might add. There was no need for them to throw me onto the sidewalk the way they did, but I understand their testosterone levels, I'm sure, are quite high, and after all I've done this month, I can't expect to be treated well by the police, can I?

"- So yes, back to Jenna, well, I thought we were getting along great while she was showing me all these places, and I'm certain she was being extra charming when she did her sales pitch for each place, but it was after I agreed to the last one and we filled out some paperwork, and I gave her a check I asked her for a drink to celebrate. She said she did not know but would look at her schedule, then excused herself and asked to use the bathroom. I, unfortunately, put my ear to the door and could hear her talking to someone on her phone, and she said, 'Can you believe this little creep is asking me to go for a drink?' Then she followed up with, 'No, of course not, I already have his check.' And so, she made the list. It took me about four months to act on that one and be able to get the shot off, but I did. After Heather Mills, I knew my time was limited, so I started working as fast as possible."

Milo didn't even wait for a response or a question from Jessica; he just continued.

"Next of course, was Madison O'Neil, and she, oh my god, she must have been the most beautiful of them all, such a beautiful woman, so I had given Madison two violin lessons, turns out she was quite good to begin with, she wanted to learn from me because we both happen to be left-handed. We only had two lessons before I, of course, made the desperate mistake of asking her for a date. I, I couldn't resist, and unfortunately, when she said no, I asked again as she packed up her violin, and then a third time as she was leaving, and that's when she sealed her fate. She turned and with a smile on her face, laughed and said much louder than before, 'No, absolutely not, I do not find you attractive in the least and I would never date you!' and so I stalked her for a while, learned how she moved around the city and shot her about a block or so from her apartment with my crossbow."

"And the next on your list was Angela DelVecchio?" Jessica asked.

"No. No, I did not go in list order; I went in convenience order. I currently have a list of twelve, and I would investigate them all simultaneously and, for speed's sake, target those that were most convenient; that's why I haven't made it out of Manhattan yet; it's all about convenience."

"Ahh, I see. The Upper East Side, then downtown, then the West Side, it makes sense," Jessica replied.

"Sense?" Milo scoffed, "None of this makes sense, Jessica. I am murdering innocent women for rejecting me; I do not think it makes any sense at all."

Everyone paused momentarily, and then Jessica just said Angela's name. "Angela Delvecchio?"

"Angela DelVecchio, ooh she was a tough one, she was, as you know, a beautiful little Italian girl, she was waiting tables at a place I went to regularly not far from the studio we practiced in, and unfortunately I couldn't help but to ask her out, she, of course, said no, so I asked again, I mean come on, she's a waitress, I would have been a good catch for this woman, but no, the third time I asked her out she got angry with me and told me to my face 'No, don't ask me again, you're not my type, I don't find you attractive, not one bit, and if you ask me again I'll make sure you never get served in here again.' Even though she was on the West Side, all I had to do was follow her home once to find out where she lived. After a couple more days of observation, I knew when she would be alone. She did not go easy though. I did not deliver a kill shot with my first attempt, and then she attacked me, and we had to fight for a bit before I knocked her out with a can of soup and then shot her a second time."

Milo paused again, took another sip of water, and then continued.

"So, back to me, back to my profile, back to why? It has all been revenge. Look at me, Jessica, Thomas, Joseph, look at me. I am a small man with a hair lip, who is today, as I sit before you, a twenty-eight-year-old virgin. I have tried for years to attract women. Still, women are simply not attracted to me. I am intelligent and talented, yet I am continuously rejected and ridiculed. I keep myself clean, I dress nicely, but no woman with any beauty will look my way. They laugh at me. They have been laughing for the last twelve to fifteen years, but no more. No, like Frankenstein's monster, I decided to inspire fear and teach these women a lesson once it was apparent that I would never inspire love. I discovered that I had the psychopathy that allowed me to do these things, and to not only revel in the hunt and the kill, but in the spectacle and notoriety of it all."

Milo smiled broadly.

"I have become in three short weeks one of the most famous serial killers to date, and I don't care about the semantics, between a spree killer and a serial killer, I now will be possibly as famous as Manson, and surprisingly, I loved every second of the hunt and have no regrets at all."

"Okay, then, Mr. Bilinski. You have been quite forthcoming. Is there anything else you would like to add?"

"I would like to thank the New York City Police Department for catching me before I killed more innocent women. I know I said I had no regrets, and I don't, not one, however, I also acknowledge my crimes were heinous and my victims were innocent except for being rude. Although I may sometimes have pushed one or two into being disrespectful, I believe scholars will find our times have made me who I am. My generation is loaded with phony virtue-signaling individuals who lack any genuine empathy or common decency. They were all rude and demeaning and, unfortunately, paid for it with their lives; many, many women never made my list because they were kind and even generous in their refusals."

***

After taking the confessions, they all broke for lunch, which they had again ordered from Neils Coffee Shop. Once they were finished, Tommy and Doreen fully processed Milo Bilinski for the homicides of the five women and brought him to central booking.

The following morning, the papers and the local and national media ran the arrest of William Tell as their headline story. However, nothing was more in-depth and detailed than the three full pages Gil Nunez delivered.

Later in the day, Jessica Lokeitz stood up in the arraignment court with confessions in hand. Tommy, the entire task force, and Gil sat on the benches behind her as they listened to Martin Rivnek enter a plea of not guilty for Milo Bilinski. This shocked everyone in attendance and put the city as a whole back on its heels.

William Tell

Chapter Twenty-Six

It took almost eighteen months for the Milo Bilinski trial to begin. During that time, the Manhattan District Attorney's Office conducted several evidentiary hearings and continued investigations.

Martin Rivnek was retained as Milo's counsel throughout the thirty-four-day trial. During this time, Milo received exactly what he wanted.

The weeks leading up to the trial, the trial itself, and its aftermath were a media circus. The world watched, eagerly awaiting the drama of one of the 'trials of the century' to unfold. The most prolific spree killer in modern history played games with the system. He used his lawyer as a stooge, quasi-representing himself with constant outbursts and arguments, constantly avoiding and rejecting his counsel's recommendations.

Milo and Rivnek called every detective and police officer involved with the case to take the stand. They even called witnesses the prosecution hadn't called, witnesses who appeared to be there to bolster the prosecution's case.

William Tell

It became quite clear to Jessica Lokietz, the rest of the District Attorney's Office, as well as the presiding judge, the Honorable Hammond Riccard, that the defendant, Milo Belinski, was not seeking an acquittal in this trial but was instead seeking the attention and notoriety of being the most notorious spree serial killer in modern history.

Milo asked the same question to Tommy and each of the other detectives assigned to the Task Force while they were on the stand: if they knew of a more prolific serial killer in New York City than himself, since Joel Rifkin. He also noted several times that he had killed more women than David Berkowitz, who had killed six people and wounded seven others.

He also badgered Officer Tony Ramirez, a weightlifter, who at five foot ten and two hundred and thirty pounds was almost twice Milo's size, why he had thrown him to the sidewalk in such an aggressive manner, when Ramirez replied, "I had to act quickly for the safety of myself and my partner." Milo asked if it was because he was afraid. Officer Ramirez, who stood side by side with Milo and made him look like a child with a beard, questioned the question, "Afraid?" and Milo continued, "Yes, afraid. You, Officer Ramirez, feared me. You, Officer Ramirez, knew full well what I am capable of, and you knew you and your partner were in grave danger when you approached me for arrest, is that not correct?"

Tony Ramirez, a seasoned officer who saw an opening, readily agreed with Milo Bilinski: "Yes, yes, sir, you are absolutely correct. I acted quickly and hastily because I knew how dangerous you were and desperately wanted to protect myself and my partner from you."

Milo smiled, his eyes blinking feverishly, and dismissed the witness.

Judge Riccard, on two occasions, called the defendant's council into his chambers to unequivocally state that he thought the defendant was not acting in his own interest, however, allowed the trial to proceed because it was the defendants representation of himself that was undermining his case, as well as being somewhat afraid of the media attention going against him if it were to appear he was assisting Milo in anyway, especially during an election year.

As the trial dragged on for more than a month, it became apparent that Milo Belinski was using this time in court, in front of a jury, and in front of the media, to continue his confession in greater detail and paint a larger and broader vision of his crimes for the world to see.

After the trial ended, the jury took less than four hours to convict Milo Belinski on all charges, and a sentencing date was set less than a month later.

But Milo Belinski, being who he was, had been saving something for the Judge, the media, and the world at large.

The morning of his sentencing, the court was filled with family members, the media, and the detectives involved in the case, including Tommy. When the judge handed down five sentences of life imprisonment without the possibility of parole, and all the related crimes totaling two hundred thirty-four years, Milo began to slow clap. He then thanked the judge, turned and thanked the detectives seated behind him, and briefly apologized to the family members in a rather backhanded way, "I am sorry for you, the families of my victims. I know it has been hard on you, but these girls should have been kinder."

Amidst the shock and gasps from all who attended the sentencing that day, Milo confidently turned back to Judge Hammond Riccard and said,

"Thank you, Judge Riccard, I think you have done your duty in my case, and you, sir, are a credit to the City of New York. But now that we are here, and in front of these reporters and the public, I must say it is time to make a deal."

Judge Riccard looked perplexed as he responded, and the courtroom fell silent.

"I am sorry, young man? Now is the time to make a deal? No, son, I think that time has long passed."

"I beg to differ, Your Honor," Milo replied in his usually professional and polite manner. "The jury has found me guilty, and I am, and you have passed a harsh but certainly fair sentence, one that I wholly understand and agree with."

"So, what is your point, son? What are you getting at?"

"Well, Your Honor, we have yet to determine. Well, at least, I do not know, but maybe you do? Where I will be spending the rest of my life behind bars, and here is where we can make a deal."

Judge Riccard paused for a moment, he had just spent over a month on one of the strangest cases of his career, and it now appeared there was going to be another wrinkle, but he didn't let on to his suspicions, he just asked, "What are you getting at, young man?"

"I have read up on the subject and want to go to the Otisville Correctional Facility."

"If you've done some reading on the subject, then you must realize that Otisville is a federal prison, and you, sir, will be heading to a state prison."

"Yes, I do fully realize that; however, I do believe there is always a way to make a deal, and as I mentioned a few times during our trial, I have killed more people than David Berkowitz." Milo paused for a moment, then continued, "My convictions are for five victims, there are more that are unaccounted for," then with a rather flippant bit of sarcasm he continued with, "My schedule is wide open, Your Honor, so maybe you have your people get with my people, and we'll discuss Otisville."

***

The remainder of the case was now in the hands of the District Attorney's office. Validating and investigating Milo Bilinsky's claims took weeks of negotiation.

A deal was struck once Milo convinced them he had committed two more murders and could easily clear the open cases. He would spend the rest of his life in the Otisville Correctional Facility, in Otisville, New York. Considered by many to be the easiest place to spend time in New York State for the remainder of his life.

Of course, Milo kept up his end of the bargain. He was enthralled by the fact that he got the attention and notoriety he so desperately craved. This act again threw his name into the media's limelight, and he felt as though he was gaming and beating the system, and in a way, he absolutely was.

He subsequently pled guilty to the homicide of Sonia Montoya, a twenty-seven-year-old dental technician, who, like all the others, had spurned his advances and insulted his manhood.

He had followed her from her dental office on West 58th Street into Central Park as she headed to the East Side, where she would meet her sister and catch the six-train home together.

But Milo, who followed her closely that evening quicky slit her throat from behind with a six-inch knife and left her dead on a path approaching the boat pond, which is where he discarded the knife. The Central Park Precinct had been searching for her killer for almost two years, with zero leads and zero luck, and now the case was cleared.

Milo also pleaded guilty to the homicide of Jennifer Strause, who was his first victim. he killed her almost a year before his spree was to start with Sonia Montoya. Like all the others, she insulted Milo when she spurned his advances.

Milo stalked Jennifer, an attractive and stylish young woman who was a manager at a clothing store inside the Danbury Fair Mall in Connecticut, close to where Milo grew up and his parents still lived.

Finding the apartment complex Jennifer lived in, he waited patiently one evening for her to come home alone from an evening out with friends and stabbed her eleven times.

There was a video of his attack, but he was not recognizable. When asked by detectives why he had used a knife on his first two victims and not the others, he stated:

"I did not like the knife. I had to be too close, I had to touch them, and it was terribly messy. I came up with the idea of a crossbow from watching Game of Thrones, and found one that was small, collapsible, and fit into a viola case. It was completely silent. I ordered one online and had it shipped to my parents' house in Connecticut. I loved it, it is a wonderful little weapon, and I was able to give each of those bitches exactly what they deserved."

Chapter Twenty-Seven

Before the ridiculous events of Milo Bilinski's circus trial, Tommy and the rest of the William Tell Task Force disbanded. Tommy and Doreen returned to their assignments in the 2-1 to start catching cases again.

Joe, Therese, and Miguel returned to the Homicide Task Force to assist in other large and complex cases throughout Manhattan North. Brenda and Gloria went back to the PAA office's special assignment department.

Jimmy returned to the 2-1 squad for only eight days. Before he began the Sergeant's course, the entire team took him out and had a party at Finnegan's Wake Pub on 1st Avenue, where he and Tommy had had a few too many one night during the William Tell investigation.

The William Tell Murders took a toll on Tommy, nearly breaking him several times. He knew Milo Bilinski was the monster of this story. Still, he could not help but feel responsible that four more young women lost their lives after he caught the first Heather Mills homicide.

He knew in his heart that he had done everything he could. He realized that the speed at which Belinski moved, and the lack of physical evidence were unique to this case and unlike any other case in which any of these veteran detectives had worked before. On top of the stress incurred over those three weeks, the extreme lack of sleep really did a number on him physically.

But all that aside, he felt this being his case, it was his responsibility, and the arrest and conviction of Milo Belinski was secondary to the ghosts of the five women he killed, the five young innocent women who would now forever haunt Tommy, who would always wonder if he could have done more?

Epilogue

Logan Mathews pleaded guilty to gun and drug possession and was released from Rikers Island a little more than four months after his arrest. He still lives in Queens and is still trying to become an actor; he is currently bartending in Manhattan and still sells small amounts of drugs on the side.

Hamza "Harry" Simsek pleaded guilty to possession of the knife and the drugs and was released from Rikers Island eight days after his arrest with time served.

Each of the victims' families, roommates, and friends, now live with the ghosts of their dear departed, stolen from them by a madman so early in their lives. Some attend support groups, some try to lock their memories and emotions up in a private place away from public or even private view, as for them, their grief is their own, and their losses now haunt them in their own individual ways.

Milo Bilinski was able to slither his way into the Otisville Correctional Facility, where he currently sits, often reading fan mail from twisted individuals who find a form of celebrity in serial killers. He has, to date, never shown one bit of remorse, and in fact brags about his deeds to anyone who will listen, a mistake that caused him to take the first real

Praise for the Tommy Keane Detective series:

"Detective Tommy Keane is one true-blue streetwise cop. But what makes him exceptional is his honest soul. That's a combination that can keep you turning the pages deep into the night."

- Jay Schadler, 20/20, ABC News, Nightline, Good Morning America, and National Geographic.

"From the streets of the Bronx to the Upper East Side, Sister Margaret, offers a tantalizing glimpse of NYC crime where nothing is ever what it seems, and fighting it is anything but routine."
- NYPD Police Commissioner, Dermot Shea.

"Devious intense and disturbing."   -
Zoe Williams, whatsbetterthanbooks.com   Best Book Blog 2017.

"You can't get any more New York than Detective Tommy Keane. Reading this series is like walking in the shoes, and seeing through the eyes of a man who embodies the city, nail-biting, shocking, and fascinating, these stories are the real deal - and highly addictive."

-Meg MacCary, Desperately Seeking the 80's Podcast.

"A gut punch of a tale that takes the reader behind the crime scene tape and onto an exhilarating tour of the streets, drug dens, dive bars and precinct houses of New York City, with an insiders view that rarely makes the papers."
- Jesse Smith, Crime Journalist, Kingston Times.

"The Myers Siblings create real, raw, heart wrenching crime fiction like no one else in this genre."
– Kayla Waters, True Crime Exposed Podcast.

Tommy Keane is the man! Travis and Natasha write their books in a way that makes it easy to follow yet gives you great detail and keeps you wanting more! They are absolutely my favorite crime authors of all time!
- Sam Sprunger, The 500 Section Lounge Podcast.

"NYPD Detective Travis Myers spent years "on the job" in the Bronx. Now, Travis and his sister Natasha, bring to life the escapades of fictional detective Tommy Keane in these fast-paced police procedurals."
- Peabody Award-Winning Investigative Reporter, Host of the True Crime Reporter Podcast, Robert Riggs.

"Authentic and engaging crime fiction."
– Sandra Mangan, crimefictionlover.com

"An exciting and interesting read, loaded with plot twists, consider me an official Tommy Keane fan!"
– Suzie Que, Punkoleum Magazine

beating of his life by a low-level mobster doing federal time on a racketeering case.

But all of this is still to come.

Right now, Detective Tommy Keane sleeps, hopefully well, as soon he will awaken to a new day and a new case folder, one that may become a new chapter in his story.

Read on for a sneak peek at the next book in the Tommy Keane series:

Antonio Canales

Then, just as the conversation resumed, Tommy's phone began to buzz. Not recognizing the number, he answered, "Keane here."

"Tommy… It's Terry. I need your help. The cops … detectives from your precinct picked up our Shane a little while ago. They're saying he done a murder down in Carl Schurz, saying he killed some kid by bashing his head in with a Belgian Block, We know he had nothin to do with this, but they got him, scooped him up at his apartment less than an hour ago. Are you working? Do you know anything about this?"

"No, no I'm away at the moment visiting Caitlyn. I don't know anything about this. Tell me more; tell me what's going on."

"What I told you is really all I got, a couple of detectives went by his place like forty maybe fifty minutes ago and grabbed him up. They're charging him with the murder of another kid from the neighborhood named Tony; kid was found beaten to death with a big Belgian Block, you know, a cobblestone, crushing his skull over by the Peter Pan statue in the park. Supposedly, it's a pretty bad scene."

"Fuck me, what do you know about Shane's whereabouts at the time?"